Kodiak Mysteries

Friends, Nature and Corporate Deceit

John Russell

HoJoPress Publications

ISBN 979-8-9896331-4-2 (paperback)

ISBN 979-8-9896331-5-9 (ebook)

Book Cover by Sadia Asmir

Preface

Nestled amidst Kodiak's majestic peaks and pristine landscapes, a profound narrative unfolds, one where the intertwined themes of environmental conservation and personal relationships take center stage. In "Kodiak's Mysteries," we invite you to embark on a journey where the bonds between friends and the sanctuary of nature converge into a compelling story of discovery and devotion.

Here, amidst the ancient trees and clear streams, a dedicated group of friends unearths the mysteries beneath this tranquil wilderness's surface. What begins as a desire to protect the natural wonders of Kodiak becomes a profound testament to the enduring strength of personal relationships.

In the heart of this tale, the beauty of the environment serves as more than just a backdrop; it is a character unto itself, a living, breathing entity that binds our protagonists together. Through their eyes, you will witness the staggering importance of safeguarding our planet and how their quest for truth resonates with the larger conservation mission.

In a world where human connections often unravel, "Kodiak's Mysteries" showcases the power of unity, friendship, and a shared passion for protecting our planet's most cherished places. As you journey with our characters through heartwarming and challenging times, you will understand the inextricable link between preserving nature and strengthening personal relationships.

"Kodiak's Mysteries" explores the equilibrium between humanity and nature and how personal connections and the environment shape our world. It is a story that dares to ask us to appreciate and protect the Earth's wonders while celebrating the ties that bind us all together in a world that sometimes seeks to keep us apart.

To my daughter Rebeccah, this book is dedicated to you in appreciation of your unique presence and love for people and nature.

I love you

Contents

Chapter 1

I'm wrapping up my final tasks at the bustling office, where the hum of fluorescent lights and the tap of keyboards echo. Tomorrow marks the beginning of my vacation as I escape to Kodiak, a mountain community promising relief from the corporate whirlwind. The demands had been relentless, and this much-needed vacation was like a lifeline.

Exchanging weary smiles and nods with my co-workers as I turned off my computer. Carla, my dedicated assistant, passed by with a knowing look. "Counting down the hours, Rebeccah?" she quipped, her voice tinged with playful sympathy.

I laughed. "More like minutes."

Her eyes crinkled in amusement. "You deserve this break. The team can handle things here."

"Thanks, Carla. I'm leaving things in capable hands." I appreciate her reassurance and her unspoken understanding of our pressures.

Walking to the breakroom, I bumped into Mark, the innovative head of product development. His eyes sparkled with curiosity. "Kodiak, right? Your escape begins tomorrow?"

Replying, relief evident in my tone. "It's time to trade the boardroom for the mountains."

Mark chuckled. "You've earned it. Hey, don't forget to bring back some fresh ideas."

"You understand me too well," I quipped, appreciating his unwavering support for blending business with pleasure.

Heading to my office's exit, I ran into Emily, a vibrant graphic designer. She grinned. "Leaving us for the mountains, Rebeccah? Can't say I blame you."

Laughing. "It's temporary, I promise. I'll be back with a tan and renewed energy."

"I'll hold you to that," Emily winked.

Exiting the office, I noticed a lightness that had been absent for too long. The night air was cool, and the city lights cast a glow. My phone buzzed with a text from Samantha: simple "Counting down!". The message brought a smile to my lips. Her excitement was infectious.

The night air was cool and refreshing, a welcome departure from the office's air-conditioned confines. The faint scent of nearby food trucks, intermingled with the aroma of blooming flowers, created an urban sense.

I found my car. It was a reliable companion, seeing me through countless late night conversations. Unlocking the doors, I slid into the driver's seat, the leather yielding beneath me.

The car hummed, marking my shift from work to personal time. Dashboard lights illuminated the space, casting a serene glow. Navigating traffic, the city's vitality enveloped me. Music filled the air as I drove past familiar sights, basking in Sunnyville's evening charm. The sun painted the sky in vibrant hues, a mesmerizing sight. Grateful for the respite, I turned towards home, content and at peace.

Walking through the door of my home, I was glad the day's demands had lifted from my shoulders. The inviting warmth of the interior embraced me. I kicked off my shoes near the entryway, and a sense of relief washed over me—the first step to unwinding after a long day.

With a contented sigh, I walked into the living room, my steps echoing against the hardwood floors. The promise of a quiet evening ahead was a comforting thought. In the kitchen, I retrieved a bottle of red wine from the cabinet and poured myself a glass. The rich aroma filled the air. My thoughts turned to the task at hand—packing for my upcoming trip to Kodiak. The suitcase stood in the middle of the room. I opened the suitcase and looked through my dresser for something to put inside.

"I don't want to do this right now. This can wait until morning," I told myself, closing the suitcase and placing it at the foot of my bed.

I entered the living room and settled onto the couch, my body sinking into the plush cushions. Samantha agreed to accompany me on the drive to Kodiak. A familiar warmth spread within me as I thought about the journey ahead.

I reached for my phone and dialed her number. The phone rang, and her voice on the other end carried the comforting cadence of familiarity.

"Hey, Sam," I greeted, a smile forming as her voice greeted me in return.

"Hey, Rebeccah! Are you thrilled about our road trip?" Samantha's enthusiasm was infectious.

"You understand I'm still knee-deep in the pre-trip chaos," I confessed with a chuckle.

Samantha laughed. "Tell me about it. My suitcase is giving me the stink eye right now."

Sharing a laugh, I commented, "Mine is just sitting on my bed, waiting to come to life."

"Let's make a deal," Samantha suggested. "We'll tackle the packing tomorrow morning together. Deal?"

"Deal," I agreed. The idea of conquering the task alongside Samantha made it seem less daunting.

"I need this trip," I told my trusted friend. "I am stuck in a rut and need a fresh perspective to get me going again."

"I know what you mean," Samantha commented. "A break will do me good as well. I can't wait to see Kodiak."

I leaned back on my couch, tasted my glass of wine, and said, "I will see you tomorrow."

"You sure will. I will be there bright and early. I have made a playlist for the ride there. You can never have too much music!" She said with enthusiasm.

"Have a wonderful night," I mentioned.

She let out a sigh and said, "You too!"

I hung up the phone and took another sip of my wine. The last drops of my favorite Merlot. The dry wine lingered in my glass, a final sip of relaxation before the evening's end. I set the empty glass on the coffee table, a gentle clink punctuating our talk's lightheartedness.

The room bathed in the dimmed lights, creating an atmosphere of tranquility as day surrendered to the night. Rising from the couch, I stretched my arms overhead. The journey to Kodiak was on the horizon, and a cherished friend made the excitement more apparent.

The bedroom beckoned its cozy embrace, a welcome haven. The sheets and plush pillows comforted me as I slipped into bed. Gazing up at the ceiling, the workday replayed in my mind like scenes from a movie. I needed this trip. A smile formed on my face after leaving town to relax.

The first rays of morning light filtered through the curtains, and the gentle chime of my alarm clock marked the beginning of a new day. With a groan, I reached over to silence the persistent sound, my hand fumbling before finding its mark. The room was infused with a tranquil environment, and the dawn painted a serene scenery within the confines of my bedroom.

Stretching, I threw off the covers and swung my legs out of bed. I rose from the bed, my steps purposeful as I went to the bathroom.

I splashed my face with cool water. The sensation was invigorating. A subtle jolt roused my senses. I dried my face with a towel, the plush fabric absorbing the moisture. The routine was familiar, much like when I went to the office. Though nothing similar, I was finally feeling a little lighter than before.

The closet and its contents were a realm of endless choices. Amongst the possibilities, I settled on an ensemble promising comfort and style—a pair of shorts and a t-shirt. My fingers brushed through my hair, coaxing it into place. The vibrant red strands caught the morning light, casting a fiery halo around my face.

With a final touch of lip gloss, I was ready. I went to the kitchen, the wooden floor cool beneath my feet. A knock resonated through me. Setting aside my breakfast plate, I went to the door. The morning light spilled into the entrance, illuminating the figure before me. Her petite frame and blonde hair caught the sunlight, and her brown eyes twinkled with mischief which defined her.

Dressed in a casual yet chic ensemble, Samantha exuded a sense of confidence that was her own. A light denim jacket draped over a white T-shirt. Distressed jeans and ankle boots completed the outfit, evidence of her knack for combining comfort and style.

The realization dawned on me again—Samantha was a mystery to many. Despite our close friendship, her work remained unknown. Rumor said she was a white hat hacker, but her role and organization remained guarded - a compelling puzzle, adding an air of intrigue to her persona.

"Ready for our adventure?" Samantha's voice was a cheerful melody, her words carrying a contagious excitement that matched mine.

I replied, my smile reflecting our enthusiasm. "You look as radiant as ever."

Samantha laughed at the sound, a blend of joy and playfulness. "Radiant, huh? You sure comprehend how to make a girl feel important."

Sharing a laugh was a ritual as familiar as the sunrise. The road ahead held a different adventure, promising breathtaking sites, laughter, and the joy of exploring the unknown together.

Samantha and I stood in my bedroom, the open bag before us. I folded a sweater and placed it in the luggage. The garment held echoes of cozy evenings by the fire and brisk mountain air. Samantha's voice filled the room as she debated the merits of bringing an extra pair of hiking boots. Her words were a playful dance of practicality and spontaneity, evidence of her vibrant spirit. Laughter accompanied her musings, a reminder this journey was not about the destination but the moments along the way.

We selected clothing and accessories, and I was ready for adventure. We made our way out of my house and to my car. We merged onto the road. Trees lined the roadside, their leaves dancing in the breeze. The open sky stretched overhead, mirroring the excitement building within us. The sound of tires against the pavement was rhythmic.

"I can't believe we're finally on our way," I remarked to Samantha.

She nodded in agreement, "I'm right there with you. I've been looking forward to this break. I'm eager to soak in all the beauty Kodiak has to offer, especially the tranquility of nature. Remind me again, where are we staying?"

"We'll be at the Evergreen Haven Lodge," I explained. "It comes highly recommended, with its rustic charm and all-inclusive amenities. A colleague suggested it, and the online reviews are highly rated. Plus, there are many hiking trails and other activities to enjoy."

"Sounds like the perfect spot to unwind and let all the stress fade away," Samantha remarked with a smile.

Mountains loomed in the distance. As the hours rolled by, the scenery shifted, and the mountains drew closer. The town is between the mountains, in the valley, a scenic haven taken from the pages of a storybook. The streets lined with charming storefronts, their facades inviting us to explore and discover the heart of this mountain community.

Parking the car along the quaint street, the sun-warmed pavement.

'It's good to stretch our legs,' Samantha said.

I looked at Samantha, "Do you want to go ahead and explore? We still have time before we can check in to the resort."

Samantha responded, "Sounds like a great plan. I love the store and shops. It looks like something from a movie."

The buildings that lined the streets with intricate details are proof of the town's rich history and vibrant spirit. Colorful banners fluttered in the breeze, celebrating community events and gatherings. People strolled by, some with dogs on leashes and others with backpacks over their shoulders.

The car doors clicked shut behind us, and the storefronts lining the street caught our attention, each exuding its unique charm. One name stood out—"Rustic Artisan Emporium." Its wooden facade radiated warmth, inviting us to step inside and explore. The window display was a captivating collage of colors and textures. There were handcrafted textiles in earthy tones, delicate pottery, and designed jewelry that sparkled like hidden gems. Each item held a piece of Kodiak's spirit, an invitation to immerse ourselves in the local artistry.

"Shall we step inside?" Samantha asked, her voice suggesting a sense of adventure.

I looked at her and smiled. "Sure!"

The bell above the door tinkled as we stepped into the store. Greeted by the soothing scent of wood and the inviting tone. The interior was a cozy haven showcasing the handcrafted treasures lining the shelves and display cases. A friendly smile from behind the counter drew our attention. The store's attendants, cheerful women with a genuine aura of welcome, stood ready to assist us. Samantha and I exchanged glances.

"Welcome!" the store attendant chimed, her voice as welcoming as the atmosphere around us. "Is there anything specific you're looking for today?"

I smiled in response, appreciating the warmth of their hospitality. "We're just taking in the beauty of your store," I replied. "The craftsmanship here is incredible."

The other attendant, arranging a display of hand-painted ceramics, beamed. "Thank you so much! We're fortunate to work with such talented local artisans."

Walking along the shelf, Samantha stopped and felt some of the locally woven textiles. "Are many of these items made by artists from Kodiak?"

The first attendant nodded. "We're proud to show artists' work from our town and nearby communities. Every item here has its unique tale, crafted with love and dedication."

We admired a hand-carved bear, and the attendant shared its intriguing backstory, "This bear was carved from a log struck by lightning about 4 months ago. You can still see some of the discoloration from the strike, adding to its beauty."

"Wow," I exclaimed. "It's truly stunning."

"If you're interested, there's an art fair coming up in a couple of weeks," another attendant said, handing Samantha a flier. "You can hear their stories firsthand. People come from miles around for it."

"Thank you so much," Samantha replied, taking the flier from the cashier. "I'd love to come back and experience it."

We left the store, and our eagerness encouraged us to explore further. Walking down the street, Samantha and I exchanged excited glances. The atmosphere was serene, and tranquility hung in the air. The mountains loomed in the background, their majestic presence a reminder of the adventures awaited us. The streets bustled with the activity of locals going about their day and tourists.

Samantha and I spotted a quaint coffee shop and made our way inside. The interior was a haven of coziness, with plush chairs and rustic wooden tables. The counter, adorned with chalkboard menus displaying various creations and pastries, drew our attention.

"Welcome!" greeted one of the baristas behind the counter. "What can I get started for you?"

"I'll have a cappuccino," I ordered.

She asked Samantha, "And what can I get for you?"

"I'll have the same thing," Samantha replied.

"Great choice! Two cappuccinos coming right up," the barista said eagerly.

We paid for the drinks and left the shop. We settled into the car again. The drive towards the Evergreen Haven Lodge was spectacular. We passed meadows, their vibrant green contrast against the clear blue sky. The lodge's rustic exterior blended seamlessly with its natural surroundings. The sight demonstrated the town's commitment to preserving its natural beauty and celebrating its artistry.

The lodge's lobby, with wooden beams overhead, exuded a timeless charm, and the flickering glow of a stone fireplace added a cozy touch. We stepped into the lobby, and our footsteps echoed against the polished wood floors, creating a rhythm harmonizing with the lodge's heartbeat. Samantha and I exchanged smiles as we checked in. The lodge's staff extended the same hospitality we encountered throughout Kodiak.

Walking down the lodge's hallway, a murmur of voices reached our ears, drawing our attention toward an ajar door. Something was happening inside the conference rooms. The sign at the entrance announced it was a community meeting, and all were welcome. The speaker's voice rose above the hushed conversations. With a subtle nod, we reached an unspoken agreement – we wanted to listen in, to catch a glimpse of the conversation unfolding within the meeting room.

My gaze was drawn to the stage. A tall, slender figure radiated confidence. There was Elena Vega, an environmental activist. Dressed in earthy tones that mirrored the natural world.

She addressed the crowd, "Undeveloped land is like a home for many different plants and animals. Building things on that land can mess up their homes and make it harder for them to survive. Some animals might even be in danger of disappearing forever. We don't want that to happen in Kodiak or anywhere. Businesses need to respect the land and its natural resources."

I leaned over to Samantha and commented, "I had never thought about the animals and other ecosystems. My life is in the marketing world, and progress is key, but listening to Elena made me think. Am I a caretaker of the land? Do my actions matter that much?"

Samantha started, "If we don't take care of the land, then it will be just one big city. Look at our surroundings. It would be a shame not to have this around for future generations."

I looked around the room at others. People hung on to her every syllable, their reactions ranging from nods of agreement to expressions of awe. Elena Vega was a driving force for change, and she could inspire even the most apathetic heart. Applause, nods of agreement, and the occasional glance all testified to the resonance of her message.

Elena's talk revealed a path I had always yearned to walk but hadn't found. The sincerity in Elena's voice and the authenticity of her experiences turned abstract ideals into tangible possibilities. My gaze remained fixed on Elena throughout the message.

The event drew close, and the ethical dilemmas surrounding corporate pursuits in such pristine surroundings gained a renewed urgency.

"I need to think about this more seriously," I said. "If we don't preserve the earth now, my grandchildren won't know the beauty of Kodiak or any other natural place."

Samantha nodded. She turned to me with a smile. "It's been an incredible day."

Nodding, my gaze still lingering on the breathtaking scenery. "Today was more than I could have imagined."

Samantha's eyes twinkled with mischief. "I don't know about you, but I'm ready to freshen up before dinner. Shall we head to our rooms?"

"That sounds like a great plan."

We left the lodge's common area and headed down the lit hallway. The rustic charm of the lodge's interior continued to cast its spell. The wooden beams overhead created an inviting atmosphere. The soothing sounds of nature seeped in from the open windows.

Samantha's eyes sparkled with excitement and contemplation. "Isn't Kodiak just breathtaking? The way the mountains and surroundings cradle the town is like a haven."

I nodded, turning to the window. "The town and the wilderness blend so seamlessly."

"Can you imagine this place being developed into something more commercial? It's already perfect– a true sanctuary," commented Samantha.

My expression mirrored her concern. "I agree. The way the lodge nestles within the mountains, it's like it belongs here, a part of the backdrops. Developing it further would risk losing its natural harmony."

We arrived at our rooms. My gaze fell on the cozy bed with its plaid-patterned quilt, a wooden desk adorned with a vase of wildflowers, and a window that framed a view of the towering pines outside.

The room seemed to breathe with the spirit of Kodiak, and I couldn't help but smile. After a refreshing shower, I glanced in the mirror. I couldn't deny that the day's experiences left an indelible mark on me. With a final spritz of a delicate fragrance, I was ready to join Samantha and begin an adventure in Kodiak.

Chapter 2

The room was much like Kodiak's beauty. Woven with earthy tones, a plaid-patterned quilt on the bed paid homage to the wonders outside. Wildflowers decorated the desk by the window, their delicate petals reflecting the colors of the nearby meadows.

A contented smile graced my lips. This place touched something deep within me, a connection I hadn't expected. It stood in stark contrast to my life in the corporate world, where the urban hustle and bustle often drowned out the whispers of nature.

I had never considered myself an advocate for environmental causes, but Elena's message the previous day left a mark on me. The lodge's untamed surroundings ignited a desire to become a steward of this untouched land.

I have always been a corporate woman, driven by the demands of my career. Gazing out the window, I loved the beauty of Kodiak and could not imagine tall buildings and homes everywhere.

I approached the dining room, and the enticing aromas of breakfast greeted my senses. The room was bathed in soft, warm light courtesy of wrought-iron chandeliers that hung overhead. A breakfast buffet at the room's heart spoke of comfort and culinary artistry. Baskets brimmed with baked pastries. A display of seasonal fruits showcased the vibrant colors of nature, while bowls of creamy oatmeal promised warmth and nourishment. An assortment of artisanal bread and cheeses added to the array is evidence of the lodge's commitment to celebrating flavors.

I filled my plate with a bowl of oatmeal with fresh, plump berries, a slice of hearty whole-grain bread, and a selection of sourced cheeses.

I approached a table where the morning sun spilled in. Two individuals were already seated. The man with dark hair framed his face. His attire blended rugged functionality with casual elegance, like he was ready for a long hike through the woods, embodying the Kodiak spirit. His coat looked like it had weathered numerous outdoor adventures, suggesting a life connected to the wilderness.

The woman exuded an air of focus and composure. Her attire seamlessly combined professionalism. She was calm and had shoulder-length blonde hair.

I stumbled upon a serendipitous meeting. I couldn't help but reach the table with apprehension as if my footsteps on the floor were almost tentative. The slight quiver in my voice betrayed my anxiety.

"Excuse me," I began, "Is this seat taken? May I join you?"

The man smiled friendly and gestured to the empty chair. "Of course, please, have a seat."

The woman, her attentive green eyes fixed on me, nodded with a friendly demeanor. "You're more than welcome. I'm April, and this is Seth."

A sense of relief washed over me as I settled into the offered seat. "I'm Rebeccah. Nice to meet both of you. It's such a beautiful morning, isn't it?"

Seth nodded, his eyes gleaming with enthusiasm. "The view from here is stunning."

April concurred, "Indeed. It's one of my go-to spots for relaxation."

"I can't imagine getting any work done with this view. I'd be mesmerized by it all day," I remarked.

Turning the conversation, April asked, "Did you catch Elena's talk yesterday?"

"Yes, I did. It was incredibly inspiring, especially for someone like me who's more accustomed to city life," I replied.

Seth's spoke. "That speech by Elena was inspirational for many of us. Corporations like Kensington Corporation want to develop the land."

Samantha walked into the dining room. Seth immediately stopped talking. Their gazes locked, and a knowing smile graced Seth's lip, acknowledging their unspoken bond. Samantha's eyes flicked in my direction in that same heartbeat. It was a subtle, almost imperceptible movement, but it spoke volumes. At that glance, she conveyed her interest in Seth, and I couldn't help but sense the undercurrents of attraction that swirled around them.

"Hi, I'm Samantha," she said, her gaze locked onto Seth's. "It's a pleasure to meet you both."

Seth shook her hand, his own eyes reflecting a growing fascination. "This is April, and I'm Seth. Please, have a seat."

She settled into the chair. Samantha's eyes continued to gravitate toward Seth and their undeniable chemistry.

I mused, "I've never been much of an environmentalist, but being here makes me want to contribute to preserving this beauty."

April chimed in. "You're not alone. I've been covering Kensington Corporation's activities for a while now, and it's clear that their intentions are far from preserving this environment."

Seth nodded in agreement. "That's why I'm here," he explained. "I've been working on initiatives to protect Kodiak's wilderness. We need more support and more awareness."

The clock ticked on. "I hate to leave such an engaging conversation," he excused himself, "and I need to attend a gathering at the square. It's a chance to connect with more like-minded individuals and spread awareness."

April nodded in understanding. "Go ahead. We'll catch up later. Samantha, Rebeccah, it's been wonderful meeting you both."

"Excuse me, I need to review some investigation notes," April explained before leaving Samantha and me alone at the table.

"It was fun meeting you, April," I said.

April responded, "The pleasure was all mine."

Samantha leaned in; her eyes fixed on me. There was a spark of excitement in her brown eyes, and a playful smile played on her lips. "I think," she began, her voice filled with enthusiasm, "Seth is intriguing, don't you think?"

Smiling in response. "He does seem like a passionate and interesting person," I agreed.

Her smile widened as she continued, her voice a touch conspiratorial. "He's speaking at the meeting today. Why don't we attend? It's a great opportunity to get acquainted, don't you think?"

"I take it you're up for crashing the environmental speech? How romantic." I teased.

Samantha grinned, responding, "Absolutely! I'm curious about his perspective. Elena's talk got to me, so I'm keen to see where he stands. Plus, if it gets personal, I'm all in."

I nodded. "You're right, Samantha. Let's go."

Samantha's eyes sparkled. "Perfect!" she exclaimed. "Let's finish our breakfast and get ready. It's going to be an exciting day."

We finally arrived at the town square. Charming, small-town buildings surrounded the area, their facades with colorful banners and signs. Market stalls offering produce, artisanal crafts, and information about various initiatives. It was a vibrant display of community spirit and activism. A makeshift stage stood erected in the square's center. The backdrop for his speech was towering mountains framing the scene, their snow-capped peaks reaching into the cerulean sky.

Seth spoke passionately to the crowd, emphasizing, "The dangers to Kodiak's wilderness are significant and must not be overlooked. Kensington Corporation's actions jeopardize our fragile ecosystem, threatening habitat and causing pollution. We must take immediate action to safeguard our land and its inhabitants."

Turning to Samantha, I whispered, "He's echoing Elena's sentiments. Looks like ecosystem preservation is a major concern in conservation circles."

Samantha nodded, adding, "True, but what about preserving natural resources?"

Seth continued, "I'd like to share a story that shows Kodiak's wilderness's beauty and resilience. Last summer, I witnessed one of nature's most spectacular events: the salmon run."

I turned to Samantha and asked, "The salmon run? What's that?"

Samantha responded, "A salmon run is when thousands swim upstream to their spawning grounds. It's an incredible sight. They can even swim against the rapids."

"Wow," I remarked. The only thing I knew about Salmon was how to order it off a menu.

Seth continued to address the crowd, "It's a scene straight out of a nature documentary, yet it's happening right here in our backyard. That's why it's so crucial for us to protect these habitats. The salmon run not only sustains the wildlife that calls Kodiak home but also plays a vital role in the delicate balance of our ecosystem. By preserving these rivers and the surrounding wilderness, we ensure that future generations can witness the awe-inspiring salmon run and all it represents."

I glanced at Samanth and gave her a wink. She was hanging on to every word Seth was.

"Ladies and gentlemen, we must recognize our crucial role in preserving this precious land for generations. We have the power to make a difference through community-driven initiatives that directly address our environmental challenges.

One such initiative is our River Clean-Up Days. By coming together to clean up our rivers and streams, we improve water quality and enhance the health of our aquatic ecosystems. This means healthier habitats for diverse wildlife and a better environment. Our Habitat Restoration Projects are key to restoring degraded habitats and promoting biodiversity in our area. By replanting native vegetation, restoring wetlands, and creating wildlife corridors, we can ensure that Kodiak's natural habitats thrive. These projects benefit our local wildlife and provide us with opportunities for recreation and connection with nature.

Together, through initiatives like these, we can make a real difference in protecting Kodiak's wilderness and ensuring a sustainable future for our community. I urge all of you to join us in these efforts."

His words resonated with me, striking a chord that echoed the internal turmoil I had grappled with since my arrival in Kodiak. It was evident that Seth's words left an indelible mark on many, just as they had on me.

Samantha said loud enough for those around her to hear, "I had no idea Kodiak was home to such natural wonders."

Seth smiled warmly in agreement, replying, "Indeed, there are many more to discover. I barely scratched the surface today. Exploring them all would take us days."

Feeling inspired, I said, "It's sparked my desire to get involved long-term. I can envision a public service announcement promoting these initiatives. It could benefit not just the people of Kodiak but also those in the surrounding areas."

Seth shifted the focus. "I've been trying to research Kensington's activities," Seth admitted, his voice tinged with urgency. "There are unconfirmed rumors of expansion plans, and if they turn out to be true, it could have dire consequences for our surroundings. There are also whispers about EarthGuard Industries, a rival corporation, filing a lawsuit against Kensington for alleged environmental law violations. They will also begin an investigation into Kensington Corporation and its practices. There are even rumors of a potential media campaign against Kensington."

Samantha chimed in, her tone reflecting her readiness for action. "This sounds like something we can dig into quickly."

Seth puzzled. "How?"

Samantha's reply came with a mischievous glint in her eye. "I would tell you, but I'd have to shoot you. One of my rules: don't ask where the information comes from."

"She's not kidding," I couldn't help but laugh.

Samantha continued, her enthusiasm undiminished. "We should get the others involved."

I nodded in agreement.

Seth appeared intrigued but perplexed. "Others?"

Teasing. "Oh, you'd be surprised at what we can uncover when we join forces." Samantha's excitement was contagious. "Let's give them a call!"

The walk to the coffee shop was short, and as we entered, Seth took the lead, approaching the counter where a barista stood, ready to take our orders. Seeing a display case filled with delectable treats and the warm scent of baked goods wafting through the air, my senses tantalized.

"May I take your order?" the barista inquired.

"Yes, please. I'll have a creamy latte, an iced tea, and a bold Americano," Seth requested.

"Sure thing," the barista replied with a smile.

Excited, I reached into my bag and retrieved my phone. With a sense of anticipation, I first dialed Breanna's number. The phone rang, I couldn't help but smile, knowing that our little group was about to embark on a new and meaningful adventure.

Breanna answered with her usual enthusiasm, "Hello, Rebeccah! What's going on? Are you having a great time in Kodiak?"

Chuckling at her boundless energy. "Breanna, you won't believe what's going on here. I've crossed paths with remarkable individuals, including an environmentalist, Seth, and a dedicated journalist, April. We're on the brink of something significant!"

Breanna's curiosity was unmistakable. "Oh, do spill the details! You have a knack for finding yourself in the most intriguing situations."

I began narrating our encounter and the mounting concerns surrounding Kensington Corporation. Breanna's interest grew. She had always championed a noble cause.

"Is Samantha with you?" Breanna inquired.

With a hint of laughter, Samantha said, "Fear not, Breanna. I'm very much here."

A smile tugged at my lips. "Hold a moment; I will bring Holli into the conversation."

Initiating a three-way call, connecting Holli to our ongoing discussion. Her cheerful voice filled the line, "Hey, Rebeccah!"

"Are you willing to join us here in Kodiak for a thrilling escapade?" I couldn't help but smile.

Samantha and I took turns updating Holli and Breanna about our meeting with Seth and April and our objective to unveil the truth about Kensington Corporation's actions in Kodiak.

Holli responded, "I'm all in, as usual! My investigative skills are ready to roll. Let's dive right into this!"

With the warmth of our friendship, I introduced Seth to the group, "Alright, everyone, say hello to Seth Donavan, the remarkable environmentalist I was just telling you about. He's the driving force behind this movement."

We discussed our latest adventure, from when I arrived in Kodiak to the chance meeting with Seth and April. Breanna, the optimist, encouraged our pursuit of uncovering Kensington Corporation's activities. With her curiosity and enthusiasm for investigation, Holli was eager to dive into this new challenge.

"We need to get back to the lodge," Seth said.

Samantha commented, "Yes, we should be getting back. It has been a full day,"

Seth looked at us and said, "I do need to tend to some things away from the lodge, but I am committed to seeing this through and to making sure that Kensington does not grab any land from the residents of Kodiak."

We ended the call. Samantha and I prepared to leave the town square. On our drive back to Evergreen Lodge, we experienced a gentle rustling of leaves in the evening breeze. It was within this serene setting that Samantha's keen eyes spotted Seth in the lobby. Their gazes locked. Samantha turned to me with a warm smile.

"Rebeccah," she began, "I'll catch up with you tomorrow. There's something I'd like to discuss with him. I'll fill you in later, okay?"

I nodded. I understood their connection. "Of course, Samantha."

Samantha made her way toward Seth. The two were engrossed in conversation before disappearing into the lodge. Left alone in the lobby, I returned to my room.

The day's encounters, the serendipitous meeting with April and Seth, and uncovering the truth about Kensington Corporation's activities ignited a spark.

I entered my space and closed the door behind me. The plaid-patterned quilt on the bed, illuminated by soft lamplight, looked inviting. I settled into the room, grateful for the experiences that led me to this place. I slipped beneath the quilt, unaware of the mystery in the heart of Kodiak's wilderness.

Chapter 3

The woods, still adorned with a blanket of dew, came alive with the chorus of birds welcoming the new day. Mornings were when nature spoke in whispers, and every rustle of leaves held a secret—stepping out onto the porch. The crisp morning air greeted me with a gentle embrace. The previous day's events lingered. Kodiak captured my imagination and heart with its rugged setting.

The prospect of exploring the backcountry filled me with excitement. It is why I am to Kodiak, to be one with nature. I dressed in practical attire, opting for comfortable hiking boots, durable cargo shorts, and a moisture-wicking top. Over my clothes, I put on a lightweight jacket for the cooler forested areas.

I decided to hike alone and relish some moments of solitude. The thought of a hike by myself in the timberland was enticing. My stomach rumbled, so I walked to the dining room and enjoyed my meal.

The sun climbed higher, and I needed to go on my walk. Finishing my coffee, I left a tip for the friendly staff and stepped onto the porch. I marveled at the untouched elegance of this place. Towering trees, some ancient and gnarled, others young and reaching for the sky. Birds flitted among the branches, their songs a constant companion.

I went to the lodge's information center, a quaint cabin adjacent to the building. The center had a detailed path map on one wall. It showed different colors indicating the difficulty levels and the estimated duration of each trek. I scanned the map.

Considering my appetite and desire for a challenging walk, I settled on the Whispering Pines Trail. It is a scenic route, somewhat challenging, and about a three-hour round trip. The trailhead is nestled in a thick pine tree grove, a short drive from the resort. Getting into my vehicle, I headed towards the trailhead.

With each step, I couldn't help but think about the stories hidden in this forest. What creatures called this place home? How do we guard it from Kensington Corporation's encroachment? I couldn't fathom their desire to transform this unspoiled stretch into a realm of multimillion-dollar properties. I went into the forest, and the sights and sounds of Kodiak surrounded me.

The trail, the lush canopy above, filtered the sunlight into dappled patterns on the ground. The soft, mossy earth underfoot absorbed my footsteps, and the tranquility of the place surrounded me like a comforting embrace. It was a world apart from the bustling town square of yesterday, a world where nature held influence.

Following the path leading deeper into the forest's heart. Every twist and turn revealed something new and wondrous. Vibrant wildflowers, their colors a dazzling contrast to the verdant greenery, lined the trail. With footsteps rustling the fallen leaves, I came across a bridge spanning a small, babbling brook. Its clear waters glistened in the dappled sunlight, and I decided to pause for a moment to take in the serene charm of this spot.

A voice interrupted my reverie. "Careful. You wouldn't want to miss the best view."

I turned to the voice. It belonged to a rugged and outdoorsy appearance. A pair of binoculars hung from his neck. He had an easy, welcoming smile and the air of someone connected to the organic world.

"Hello," I greeted. I looked at him and saw the patch on his shirt showing his name. "You must be Ethan?"

He nodded, his eyes twinkling with zeal. "You must be Rebeccah, a new arrival. Seth mentioned you might be out roaming our neck of the woodlands."

"That's right. Kodiak's unspoiled splendor drew me in, and I couldn't resist looking closer." I smiled.

He gestured to the crossing. "Well, you've picked a good spot to start. It overlooks one of the most unspoiled parts. You might even glimpse our resident beavers hard at work."

We scanned the place as I joined him. Sure enough, a pair of beavers emerged within a few minutes, swimming across the still waters. It was a sight to behold, a tribute to the undisturbed nature of the landscape.

"They're fascinating creatures, aren't they?" He remarked, his eyes fixed on the beavers. "They're nature's engineers, shaping the environment to create ideal habitats for themselves and other wildlife."

I needed in agreement, captivated by the scene. "It's incredible how everything in this ecosystem is so interconnected."

Ethan smiled, his eyes overflowing with appreciation for the outdoors. "That's the charm of Kodiak. It's a delicate balance, one we work hard to protect. Seth's speech yesterday—did it resonate with you?"

"The more I learn about this place, the more I realize how important it is to guard it," I responded. "I'm eager to get involved with the initiatives Seth mentioned," I told Ethan. "I work for a marketing firm, and I want to create a PSA not just for Kodiak but also for the nearby cities to spread the message about preserving the forest instead of exploiting it for profit."

Ethan met my gaze, his blue eyes shining. "That would be fantastic. The more people who join in to protect the woods, the more families can enjoy them. Would you like to get involved directly?"

"Yes, absolutely," I replied. "I'm falling in love with this area, and the more I learn about it, the less anything else seems to matter."

"Anything else?" Ethan inquired.

I confessed, "Yes, like climbing the corporate ladder, progress—all the things my organization promotes. This feels real and beautiful. Tell me more about the ecosystems here in the forest."

Ethan's eyes widened with enthusiasm. "Of course. The ecosystems in this forest are incredibly intricate and interconnected. It's truly remarkable how everything works together to sustain life. From the rich soil to the canopy above, each part of the ecosystem supports the others in a delicate dance of life."

"That's amazing," I added. "It seems like if one part breaks, it disrupts everything."

"Exactly," Ethan affirmed. "That's why it's so important."

I felt torn between staying and leaving. I had to join Samantha back at the lodge, so I said, "Well, I need to get going, continue my hike, and rejoin the others."

Ethan smiled warmly. "Of course. It was great talking with you. I'll see you around."

"Yes, you will," I smiled back.

After bidding farewell, I continued my exploration of the backcountry. The dappled sunlight filtering through the lush canopy above created a mesmerizing play of light and shadow on the forest floor.

Wildflowers danced in the gentle breeze, and butterflies flitted from one blossom to another, adding splashes of brilliant hues to the forest's already colorful tapestry. Going farther into the woodland, the air became crisper, carrying the earthy scent of moss and pine. Birdsong saturated the air, a harmonious symphony of chirps, tweets, and melodies that serenaded my journey.

I encountered signs of the forest's inhabitants. The tracks of a deer, imprinted in the soft ground, told stories of graceful passages through the underbrush. Squirrels chattered above, their antics entertaining and reminding me I was a guest in their domain. The route led to a clear stream meandering through the area. The water was cold and sparkled in the sunlight.

I decided to return to the resort, and I retraced my steps. The path was familiar, and I moved from examining this small corner of Kodiak's wilderness.

Locating my car, I sat in it awhile to soak up the morning activities. I spent the morning discovering the beautiful setting and meeting a wonderful man. The drive back was amazing, leaving a smile on my face.

I stepped into the resort, and a sense of warmth washed over me. The interior, with timber beams and soft, ambient lighting, exuded an inviting allure that felt like coming home after a long journey. The comforting scent of pine lingered in the air, mingling with the aroma of a hearty, home-cooked meal nearby.

Samantha and Seth sat in a corner near the crackling fireplace. Their presence was a welcome sight.

Samantha greeted me with a broad smile and a playful wink. "Rebeccah, perfect timing! We've been waiting for you. Come join us."

I found one of the chairs they saved for me. The flickering flames in the nearby fireplace cast a glow over our corner, creating an atmosphere that encouraged open talk and connection.

Samantha's eyes twinkled with zeal as she spoke. "Rebeccah, you won't believe the beautiful spots we explored today."

"I just returned from a hike and met the biologist," I commented, settling into the corner with Samantha and Seth.

"Ethan?" Seth asked with a smile.

"Yes," I responded. "He's knowledgeable about everything that lives around here."

"He is," he agreed.

I nodded in agreement, and a sense of contentment washed over me. "It's remarkable how this place can captivate anyone who sets foot here."

Seth chimed in, his voice tinged with reflection: "There is a unique connection between the terrain and its people here in Kodiak. It's a bond that runs strong."

I looked at my watch.

"Any news from Breanna or Holli?" I asked, curious about our fellow adventurers.

"Nope, but it doesn't surprise me with the lack of reception out here," Samantha replied.

My phone vibrated on the table. The sound was subtle, but it distracted me from the discussion.

I reached for my phone, and my heart warmed when I saw Holli's name on the screen. Her message illuminated the screen, and it read.

Holli: "Almost at Evergreen! "

I couldn't help but smile

"Samantha, Seth," I exclaimed, "Holli and Breanna are almost here! She's just minutes away."

Samantha's eyes shone with zeal. "That's awesome! It's been too long."

About 15 minutes later, the door swung open, and Holli and Breanna stood before us with their trademark adventurous spirit and exuberant smiles. The moment they stepped inside, the energy in the room surged.

Holli's voice rang out as she exclaimed, "I can't believe we're all here. I used to come to Kodiak when I was a child. I can't remember where we stayed. Everything looks different and bigger!"

Breanna couldn't contain her joy. "It's so wonderful we are all together! The last time, we uncovered the Fredrick scandal that shook Centerville."

Holli said, "And now, we're here in the heart of Kodiak, ready to do it again."

Samantha, her mischievous glint never fading, added with a grin, "Oh, you two have no idea what we have stumbled upon!"

We began to go to the dining area to grab a cup of coffee and sit down. We found a great quiet place in the center, where I grabbed a cup of coffee for Rebeccah, and Samantha grabbed a cup of tea for Breanna.

Breanna and Holli listened. Breanna said, "Kodiak's outdoors has a way of leaving a lasting impression."

I nodded, my adventurous spirit evident. "The magnificence of this place is unlike anything else."

Samantha couldn't contain her delight as she gestured toward Seth, who stood nearby. "Ladies, allow me to introduce you to a remarkable man who's been instrumental in my Kodiak adventure."

The women turned their attention to Seth.

Breanna asked, "Samantha, how do you two know each other?"

Her eyes bright with enthusiasm, she recounted the previous day's serendipitous events.

"Rebecca and Seth were enjoying a leisurely breakfast," she began, "when Seth here caught my attention. He was talking about Kodiak's challenges from Kensington Corporation and his devotion to preserving this place struck a chord with both of us."

Holli leaned in, her eyes swelled with fascination. "So, what did you do next?"

"We stocked him and then crashed his speech in the town square," I answered, my eyes reflecting her inspiration. "It was pretty inspirational, and the Kodiak residents are behind preserving the area. There are many cool initiatives."

He said, "Yes, they are, and I want to fight to help them keep it this way."

Samantha continued, "That's when we called and invited you to come and spend some time with us. We need to find out who at Kensington is behind this to end the development."

Holli leaned forward, her eyes brimming with interest. "So after you called us, what happened?"

Seth replied, "I returned here to follow up with some people to find out if any of the Kensington Corporation came to Kodiak."

Changing the topic I inquired, "Breanna, how are the preparations coming along?"

The sentiments and sights in the room shifted as we turned our attention to Breanna and asked her about the ceremony preparations.

Breanna's eyes sparkled as she shared her vision with the ladies. "Well, ladies, picture this – our nuptials will be at a charming vineyard just on the outskirts of Centerville. You'll walk through the rows of grapevines to reach the outdoor ceremony area. There will be a rustic arch adorned with flowers under which we'll say our vows."

Samantha couldn't help but be impressed. "That sounds dreamy!"

Holli chimed in. "I bet the sunset over the vineyard will be breathtaking!"

"What about the reception?" I asked.

A mischievous grin spread across Breanna's face. "Ah, that's the best part. The reception area is in a beautiful, old barn they've converted into an event space. String lights will hang from the rafters, and we're going for a cozy, rustic-chic vibe."

Samantha's delight was evident. "That barn sounds like the perfect place to celebrate!"

Breanna nodded, "Yes, we're going for lots of blush and greenery. Roses are going to be the stars. It's been a lot of work, but I can't wait for you all to be there." The joy in her voice was unmistakable, and we couldn't help but share in her enthusiasm.

We went to our rooms. Our footsteps echoed in the cozy lodge, and the gentle flicker of lantern-style lights cast warm, inviting pools of light along the wooden corridors. Holli's eye caught sight of an old picture framed on the wall. Her gaze fixed on it before her eyes widened with recognition.

"Wait a minute," Holli exclaimed, her voice tinged with astonishment. I think I've been here before when I was a child."

Intrigued, we gathered around and examined the framed photograph depicting children, Holli among them, grinning in front of the lodge. It was remarkable how little the lodge had changed over the years.

Samantha's eyes widened with realization. "You mean you visited Evergreen Haven?"

Holli nodded, her face lighting. "Yes, I must have visited this place with my family. It's unbelievable that I didn't recognize the name of this place until now. It's like a journey back in time. This day, in the photo, it's all coming back to me."

Holli's voice turned wistful. "Ah, I remember those nights vividly," she began, a soft smile gracing her lips. "We laughed until our stomachs hurt, reminiscing about the funniest moments of our lives - like when Steve attempted to cook dinner and burned it to a crisp! We couldn't stop laughing as we tried to salvage the meal."

Our laughter filled the room as we shared similar mishaps. Holli continued, "Then there were the heartfelt stories we shared." Her gaze drifted to the photograph in her hand. "We would sit outside in the cool night air and open up about our dreams, fears, and the challenges we'd overcome."

Curious, I asked, "Was one of those dreams for you to become an attorney?"

Holli shook her head. "No way. When I was a child, my dream was to be a ballerina."

"That's every little girl's dream, isn't it?" Breanna chimed in. "It certainly was mine."

Nods of agreement circled the group as Holli returned her focus to the photo.

"And those hiking trails," she exclaimed, excitement bubbling in her voice. "Each step was an adventure, filled with breathtaking views and unexpected encounters with wildlife. I'll never forget when we stumbled upon a hidden waterfall; its cascading waters mesmerized us as we stood in awe of nature's beauty."

"It sure made an impression on you," Samantha remarked, a smile on her lips.

"Yes, it did," she exclaimed. "My parents... they mentioned something about buying land in the mountains long ago," Holli began, her voice soft and contemplative. "I never thought much of it. It was one of those family tales that never held significance?"

Her words sounded like casual dismissals from her past, an oversight that had now assumed new significance. She continued, "They always said it was an investment for the future, but it wasn't something we discussed much."

A realization began to dawn on Holli. She turned to her friends, her eyes with astonishment and enthusiasm.

She began, "I think that piece of property my parents bought... is here in Kodiak. The one they never developed."

We exchanged glances, the gravity of the situation sinking in. Kodiak has a reputation for its natural beauty, and there have been rumors about Kensington Corporation's interest in acquiring it for development. The idea that Holli's family real estate might be what Kensington was eyeing was a revelation that sent a shiver of concern down our spines.

Samantha's voice was urgent. "Holli, It might be the key to understanding Kensington's plans to acquire property and how to stop them."

Holli reached for her phone. Holli's fingers trembled slightly as she dialed the number. We gathered around, their expressions a mix of anticipation and concern.

"Hello?" Steve's voice came through.

"Steve, it's Holli," she began, her voice steady. "I need to talk to you about something important."

"Of course, Holli. What's going on?" Steve replied, his tone shifting to one of concern.

Holli took a deep breath. "Do you remember the mountain property Mom and Dad bought years ago? The one they never developed?"

A moment of silence at the other end. "Yeah, I remember. They always said it was an investment but never talked much about it. Why?"

Holli hesitated, "It may be a piece of land that Kensington Corporation is eyeing for development."

His voice tinged with nostalgia, "The property is in Kodiak. It's quite close to the lodge where we spent many summers growing up."

Holli responded, "I'm in Kodiak right now, and a situation here with Kensington. Do you know why mom and dad never developed it?"

Her brother's voice held a sense of understanding, "I think it's because Mom and Dad wanted to preserve it. They viewed it as a beautiful, unspoiled piece of real estate and wanted to keep it that way. It's what the town would want. They've always been firm about preserving the area."

Steve continued, his words heavy with concern, "It's strange that you're bringing this up now. I received a call from Joshua Peele. He says he is from Kensington Corporation. He inquired about the land and even sent a contract for us to sell it."

Holli, her eyes narrowing with resolve, asked the crucial question, "What did you tell them? Did you sign it?"

"No, I told him I wanted to talk to you first."

Holli turned her attention back to the phone, her voice earnest. "Did you receive that contract from Joshua Peele?"

On the other end of the line, Steve's voice held a note of caution as he responded, "Yes, I did. I thought it best to discuss it with you before making any decisions."

She nodded. "That's a wise choice. Could you do me a favor and email the contract to me? I want to look at it and see what exactly they're proposing."

"Of course, Holli. I'll send it right over to you. Just be cautious, okay? We don't know their intentions. We need to honor Mom and Dad in preserving the land."

Holli said her goodbyes to her brother and hung up the phone.

"Holli," Samantha began, her interest reflecting the unspoken concerns, "what if the contract offer comes with a substantial amount of money?"

She finally answered, her voice tinged with apprehension and resignation. Her eyes, once vibrant with enthusiasm, now bore uncertainty. The room held its breath as her words hung, "I don't know."

Those three words reverberated through the room, a stark reminder of the unknown course ahead. Feelings shifted from fascination to a more profound sense of contemplation.

At that moment, the room was silent, broken only by the quiet rustle of clothing and the occasional crackling of the fireplace.

Chapter 4

We huddled around the table in the common area. We were on the verge of something meaningful, and Holli's fingers, poised above the keyboard, betrayed her nervous tension. We were a few moments away from receiving the contract from her brother. The room was excited as we prepared to unravel the document's mysteries. The rustic charm of the resort provided the perfect backdrop for our meeting.

My glance shifted to Holli and then to the laptop screen, my heart keeping pace with the anxious rhythm of my thoughts. Holli's hand hovered over the mouse, and with a determined breath, she clicked to open the email containing the contract. The room held its breath as the document appeared on the screen.

I scanned the words and clauses comprising Kensington Corporation's proposal. The contract required more specificity, detailing the land's intended use and outlining the fiscal terms and the proposed deadline for acceptance. They recognized the immense possibility in the parcel of land owned by Holli's family, nestled within Kodiak.

Samantha's voice broke the stillness that settled upon us like a heavy blanket. "Holli, what does it say?"

Holli began to read aloud, her voice steady but tinged with disbelief. "Kensington Corporation proposes to purchase the property, which may secure my family's future for generations. They're offering us $5 million."

The room fell into a stunned hush. The sum was staggering, a substantial amount that might change their lives. It also underscored the gravity of Kensington's intentions. They were willing to invest a considerable sum in acquiring the property, fueling suspicions that their motives extended far beyond mere development.

Breanna was the first to break the silence. "That's an enormous offer. It makes you wonder why they're so determined to get their hands on that real estate."

I leaned forward. "We should find out when they expect us to give them an answer. Time might be a critical factor here."

"You're right, Rebeccah." Samantha agreed. "Let's not rush into this. We need to gather all the facts."

Breanna's voice carried a note of caution as she pointed out, "What happens to Kodiak if they develop it? Are they planning to preserve its natural appeal or exploit it?"

The deal offered no apparent answers to this question. We realized that Kensington Corporation's intentions might have far-reaching consequences for Kodiak's community, a place for people to vacation in a natural environment.

Putting my hand on her shoulder. "Holli, we need more facts. We must find out what Kensington plans to do with the land and how it will impact the environment and the community."

Samantha added, "Holli, we must visit this piece of property. Kensington is offering such a high price that it might be something obvious. It's time we look closer and gather as much data as possible."

The room held its collective breath as Samantha's words settled in. The prospect of visiting and venturing into the heart of this mystery caused tension and apprehension.

"I'm in complete agreement," Breanna asserted, "This is the ideal starting point."

Samantha and Holli exchanged nods, aligning with Breanna's perspective. We filed out of the resort and piled into my car. The engine roared to life. The five-mile drive seemed like a journey into the unknown and returning to familiar ground.

The highway wound through the dense Kodiak Forest, towering trees forming a lush canopy above. Sunlight filtered through the leaves, casting intricate patterns of light and shadow on the lane ahead. Sitting beside me, Holli held a folder containing the contract from Kensington.

Her eyes were on the road. We approached, revealing a breathtaking vista. It stretched out before us, a vast expanse of forest. It was a place of beauty, unspoiled by time. It sat on the edge of a lake, its waters reflecting the vibrant blue sky.

"This place is incredible," Breanna breathed from the backseat, her voice filled with awe. "It's hard to believe we might stand on the brink of its transformation."

Holli nodded, "We need to understand why Kensington wants this place. Let's explore and examine if anything obvious might explain their interest."

We embarked on a short hike down to the water. The forest surrounded us, its towering trees creating a lush, green cathedral that whispered secrets in every rustling leaf. Holli led the way, her steps purposeful as she navigated the narrow path.

The way meandered, and the lake drew nearer with each step. The sound of running water grew louder. We approached, and the trees parted, revealing a scene of breathtaking magnificence. The water stretched before us under the brilliant Kodiak sun. It was an oasis undisturbed by man's hand. The shores had smooth stones, and fallen trees transformed sculptures. A gentle breeze danced across the water, causing tiny ripples that glinted like diamonds.

Breanna's voice held a sense of wonder as she talked, "It's like stepping into a hidden paradise."

Holli's nod communicated volumes, her eyes tracing the landscape before us. "This," she whispered, her voice with awe, "is why Kensington set its sights on this real estate. It's near the highway and a water source—a developer's paradise."

My head bobbed in sync with her sentiment. "It is magnificent."

With cautious steps, we explored the area around the water. The ground was a mosaic of mossy clearings and clusters of wildflowers—as though nature had painted this place.

Our footsteps made a sound on the mossy ground as we walked. We spotted something unusual near the lake's edge. Half-buried in the soil was a metal marker. Holli knelt to examine it, her fingers brushing away the moss to reveal weathered engravings.

"It's a survey marker," she said, her voice tinged with intrigue. "This land has been surveyed."

Samantha's nimble fingers retrieved her phone, capturing a photo of the marker with a noticeable intrigue in her eyes. She mused. "Kensington conducted a survey here; it means they've got concrete plans and, most likely, the green light from somebody."

I spoke up. "We should document everything we find here—pictures, notes, and anything relevant. Samantha, can you check if there are any additional markers or signs of recent activity?"

Samantha nodded and set to work, her phone now functioning as a cyber detective tool. She scanned the area and captured images and notes of the surroundings.

Holli's glance was contemplative. "I can't help but think about my parents and why they bought this."

Sensing Holli's words, I touched my friend's shoulder.

We continued our exploration; we discovered that this land possessed all the attributes that would make it appealing for development. The scenic lake doubled as a possible resource, offering access to fresh water and pristine wilderness. The spacious and secluded land provided ample room for construction. The property boasted all the elements necessary for a lucrative development project yet also held an intrinsic value that transcended economics.

We moved closer to the lake's edge. The contrast with the corporate boardrooms and bustling streets we left behind reminded us of the preciousness of Kodiak's undisturbed beauty.

Holli's resolve was unwavering as she spoke. "We need to protect this."

Breanna contemplated the circumstance and said, "We must dig into Kensington's activities. They're targeting this real estate, and do they have similar plans for other areas in Kodiak?"

After finishing her digital documentation and placing her phone in her back pocket, Samantha agreed. "Let's head back to the resort and regroup. I'll cross-reference the data collected with recent developments in Kensington's activities."

My heart was still heavy from the discovery of the lake. Inside the car, sentiments ran deep. Samantha geared up to delve into the virtual world. Breanna busied herself sifting through the necessary details about Kensington Corporation's activities.

Holli's fingers traced patterns on the window in the front passenger seat, and her gaze was lost in the passing view. The struggle within her was apparent. She was torn between her family's economic security and the preservation of Kodiak.

She broke the calm, her voice tinged with uncertainty. "If I were to sign that agreement, it would mean a significant financial boost for my family. It's a substantial amount they're offering."

The weight of her decision hung in the air. Holli, seated next to me, exchanged a glance, and I exchanged a silent understanding that everything would be all right, no matter the outcome. Reaching out, I placed a reassuring hand on Holli's shoulder. "Holli, we understand this isn't an easy decision. Whatever you choose, we're here to support you."

Holli's eyes met mine, and there was a glimmer of gratitude in her look. "Thank you, all of you. I need to find a way to preserve it."

In the heart of the lodge's lounge, where communal warmth and coziness enveloped the furniture, the soft crackling of the fireplace further enhanced the ambiance. Seth's entrance into this sanctuary was filled with the promise of new details and connections.

"Hello, everyone!" Seth greeted us with a friendly and open-hearted tone. His question was simple. "What's new?"

"We visited Holli's parent's property," Samantha began, her voice filled with admiration. "It's stunning. No wonder Kingston has their eye on it."

"There's more," Holli added, her tone intense. "Someone's been surveying the land."

He turned his attention to Holli, his eyes flickering with recognition. "Is your brother's name Steve?" he inquired.

Holli responded with a simple affirmation, "Yes, it is."

With a contemplative nod, he continued, "I met your brother. He was here in Kodiak about a week ago. Our paths crossed in the town's diner."

The revelation sent shockwaves through our group. Holli's gaze locked onto mine, her eyes seeking answers and understanding.

"He was here in Kodiak?" her voice quivered. "What brought him here? Do you have any idea?"

Seth's demeanor was that of someone well-versed in the town's happenings. "I always keep tabs on who's around for surveying jobs."

Breanna said, "Well, now we realize where those survey flags came from."

Her voice wavered as she grappled with the revelation, "Why would he not tell me?"

I offered a plausible explanation, "Maybe he didn't want you to try to talk to him and convince him not to sell."

Holli's response held vulnerability, "He still should have told me."

Her reactions were noticeable, and her vulnerability lay bare. Her family's ownership of the property, once a guarded secret, now un-folded for all of us to witness. She appreciated the support and understanding of someone connected to Kodiak. Her family's land was a topic of discussion, and her family's history was on display.

I took a deep breath, my voice steady as I addressed my friends. "It's evident that Kensington's interest in the property isn't a coincidence. They want something in that place. We need a systematic way to arrive at the bottom of this mystery."

Samantha nodded in agreement. "We can start by researching Kensington. They must have a history of similar acquisitions and development projects. We can discover any patterns or irregularities. It might provide valuable insights."

Holli is still processing the recent developments. "I'll review the contract they offered and look for any possible traps or loopholes. Maybe that can give us a clue about what they're after, and I need to call my brother to find out where his mind is."

Seth chimed in next. "I can watch any activity. I'll recognize if Kensington starts sending personnel or equipment to the property. I'll also consult some of my contacts; some locals might have details."

I nodded. "That sounds like a solid plan. Let's also consider talking to the town historian. Kodiak has a historical society. I saw it when we were in town. They might have insights into the lodge's history and its surroundings. There may be a connection we're missing."

April walked over to join our group.

"April, Holli's brother, came to town," Seth revealed. "They surveyed the family's property. They're offering a substantial sum," he continued, glancing at the women. "It's a prime choice for developers."

I witnessed the emotions dance across April's expressive face. It was clear that this revelation caught her off guard. A growing sense of worry etched lines on her forehead, creating a subtle furrow between her brows. Her eyes, once wide with astonishment, now held a depth of understanding as if she had quickly processed the implications of this unexpected development.

Seth laid out the details, gazing at her. "We need your help with this. Your connections, knowledge, and influence can be invaluable."

April hesitated for a moment, shifting her gaze between each of us. She didn't take her decision, and her internal struggle showed. After taking a deep breath, she nodded, her voice unwavering. "All right, count me in. I'll assist you in any way I can."

April's presence altered the atmosphere, and her decisiveness proved her unwavering dedication. The relief was visible in our expressions, manifesting as subtle smiles and an almost imperceptible collective exhale.

"April, Breanna, Are you ready to go?" I asked.

They nodded, and we picked up our things and went out the door.

We drove to the Kodiak Historical Society. Breanna's knack for research and a strong eye for detail made her an invaluable asset. April's quiet demeanor left an air of mystery about her, hinting at some inner turmoil she was navigating.

We pulled into the parking lot. The quaint building exuded an air of timeless wisdom. Nestled among tall trees, it had been from another era. A sign with faded letters declared let us know we arrived.

Breanna was the first to break the silence. "Here we are," she said, her voice hinting with eagerness. "Let's hope they possess the information we need."

The interior was a veritable treasure trove of history, with shelves adorned with dusty tomes and antique relics showcased in glass cabinets. Near the entrance, a gentle-looking elderly woman was engrossed in cataloging documents at a timeworn desk.

I cleared my throat to attract her attention. "Excuse me, can you help us?"

She glanced up, her eyes twinkling with a knowing wisdom surpassing her years. "Sure, I can. My name is Joyce. How can I assist you today, dear?"

Breanna stepped forward, taking the lead. "We're here because we're interested in the history of Evergreen Haven Lodge. We hope you have some records or knowledge of its past."

Joyce's smile was warm and welcoming. "Ah, Evergreen Haven Lodge, a true gem of our town'. I do have some records and documents that might be of interest. Follow me."

We trailed behind Joyce as she led us deeper into the ranks and stacks of books, old newspapers, and magazines. The air was thick with the scent of old paper, and the soft creaking of floorboards echoed through the narrow aisles. Dust motes danced in the beams of sunlight that streamed in through the windows, creating an almost magical environment.

She stopped at a row of aged filing cabinets and began rifling through them. "Evergreen Haven Lodge has a fascinating past," she said as she pulled out a ledger. "It was one of the first lodges established in Kodiak in the early 1900s. Many prominent figures and explorers stayed during the town's early years."

Breanna's eyes lit up as Joyce handed her the ledger. She flipped through its pages, scanning the handwritten entries. "This is incredible," Breanna murmured. "It's like stepping back in time."

Breanna delved into the records and turned her attention to April and me. "Is there something specific you're looking for?" she asked kindly.

April hesitated for a moment, her internal conflict evident in her face. She said, "We're interested in any details about Evergreen Haven Lodge's ownership and any noteworthy events connecting to it."

Joyce nodded understandingly. "Ownership records might be a bit trickier, but I have some anecdotes and stories passed down through generations. Evergreen Haven Lodge has quite the past."

Breanna continued to sift through the ledger, her eyes scanning for any clues that might lead us to answers about the lodge's ownership. I listened to Joyce's stories. It emerged that navigating the secrets of Evergreen Haven Lodge would resemble unraveling a labyrinth of records.

Joyce recounted that a visionary entrepreneur named Samuel Blackstone established Evergreen Haven Lodge in the early 1900s. Blackstone had been captivated by Kodiak's undisturbed forest. The resort hosted explorers, artists, and even a few celebrities. Everyone was attracted to its rustic charm and the unspoiled magnificence of the surrounding countryside.

Breanna's sharp eye landed on an entry that caught her attention. "I think I've found something," she said, her voice tinged with excitement. "Here, it mentions a change of ownership in the 1960s. Evergreen Haven Lodge sold to Kensington Corporation."

April's eyes widened in surprise, and a noticeable tension filled the room. We exchanged glances, realizing the significance of this discovery. The puzzle pieces were falling into place, and Kensington Corporation's interest in Holli's family property had roots dating back decades.

Joyce, ever the historian, provided further context. "Yes, the sale in the 1960s was a point of contention in Kodiak then. Many locals were concerned about the lodge falling into corporate hands. They feared it would lose its connection to the community and the untouched forest that drew people here."

Breanna continued her research, digging deeper into the circumstances surrounding the sale. "I wonder if there were any protests or legal disputes related to this transfer of ownership," she mused.

Joyce nodded, "There were indeed protests and legal challenges. Some townsfolk fought to maintain Evergreen Haven Lodge as a symbol of Kodiak's natural beauty. The sale went through, and Kensington Corporation assumed ownership."

After hours of poring over historical records and absorbing the rich tapestry of Evergreen Haven Lodge's past, we thanked Joyce for her invaluable assistance. Gratitude shone in our eyes as we appreciated her willingness to share her knowledge and help us in our quest for answers.

Upon our return to Evergreen Haven, we reconvened in the lodge's great room. The room became our sanctuary, where we could gather to share our findings and scheme our next moves.

"Guess what we discovered," Breanna began, excitement bubbling in her voice. "Kensington repurchased the property in the 1960s, and it caused quite a stir."

I chimed in, "Despite protests, the sale went through."

"Kensington stepped in to refurbish the place after years of neglect," Breanna added.

"They haven't shown any interest in expanding Evergreen Haven," puzzled by Kensington's lack of interest.

We were attempting to find a motive through Evergreen Haven Lodge's past, and it was becoming evident that it had hidden secrets. Seth's area of knowledge provided valuable context, and Holli's connection to the lodge's history added a personal dimension to our investigation.

"What did you all find out," I asked, looking at Holli, Seth and Samantha.

Samantha began, "Joshua Peele has a past involvement in corporate land grabs and environmentally damaging projects. He's a key player in Kensington's expansion efforts, infamous for his ruthlessness in acquisition landgrabs."

I listened, realizing the gravity of the seriousness. Joshua Peele wasn't just a representative of Kensington; he was a linchpin in their operation, a man with a track record of exploiting natural resources.

Holli took a deep breath, her voice steady but filled with worry, as she turned their attention to the document in my hands.

"The deal," she explained, "offers an astronomical sum for our family's land, far beyond any reasonable value. It's a clear sign that Kensington has ulterior motives. They're not just interested in the property; they want it desperately."

My face was etched with worry. "What did your brother say?"

Holli responded, "My brother wants to sign the agreement."

Following Holli's announcement, April excused herself and rushed toward the guest rooms. Samantha walked Seth out to say goodbye. I glanced at Breanna and Holli.

"I've never seen Samantha so infatuated," I shared with them.

Breanna replied, "Same here. She's always composed and collected."

We all let out a soft laugh, knowing she was right.

"Holli," I said, concerned. "Why don't you go to your room and call Steve and find out why he wants to sign the contract."

"That sounds like a good idea," she said, picking up her things and leaving the room.

I glanced over at Breanna, "We need to discover Kensington's true intentions,"

She nodded, her brow furrowed. "It was quite a shock to discover that Kensington Corporation owns this, and it seems they haven't made any significant additions since. They want to expand Holli's and Steve's property and would have renovated the lodge. It's all perplexing. There's Joshua Peele. How does he fit into this puzzle?"

"I share your confusion," I replied with a sigh. "Right now, it just doesn't make sense. I have faith in Samantha's investigative skills. She always manages to unearth revelations."

Samantha waltzed into the room, her entrance accompanied by a mischievous grin. "Ah, Samantha, we're expecting nothing less than your usual hair-raising surprises," I teased, flashing a reassuring smile.

Samantha quirked an eyebrow, her eyes twinkling with mischief. "Oh, you think? Buckle up, folks, because I'm about to take you on a rollercoaster ride through the cyberspace jungle."

Breanna said, "Well, that's just what we needed – more suspense and excitement. My heart can take it, Samantha," her voice dripping with sarcasm,

Samantha laughed, a melodic sound that always lightened the mood. "Don't worry, Breanna. I promise to leave some adventure for the rest of your day. No one gets bored when I'm around!"

We couldn't help but chuckle at Samantha's playful confidence. Her enthusiasm was infectious, and we knew she'd bring a touch of adventure to our investigations, whether digital or otherwise.

I chimed in and glimpsed at Breanna, chuckling, "She's got a point!"

Delving into the investigation, Breanna couldn't resist a bit of intrigue. "By the way, Samantha, what's happening between you and Seth?"

Holli emerged from her room just in time to catch Samantha's response to Breanna's question.

Samantha's cheeks flushed with a rosy hue, her confident smile softening into a more tender expression. "You know," she began, her voice a touch quieter and more reflective. "We've been spending a lot of time together, and I think I might be a little obsessed. Maybe I might even be falling for him."

A ripple of excitement surged through the room, and the women leaned in closer. There was no way Samantha was going to escape without sharing all the delightful details of her newfound romance. Teasing grins and playful nudges accompanied their eager encouragement.

I couldn't resist a teasing remark. "Well, Samantha, it's about time! We've been waiting for this day."

Samantha laughed, sensing both flustered and thrilled by their enthusiastic response. "You all are relentless! Don't worry, you'll be the first I tell when it's official."

Breanna remarked, "Consider this payback for all the times you teased me about Aaron."

Samantha chuckled, then adopted a playful tone. "Alright, but if I tell you, I might have to shoot you."

With a collective laugh, we decided to respect Samantha's privacy. It was time to forge ahead and reveal the secrets of Evergreen Haven's past and Kensington Corporation's present.

I gazed at Holli. Her posture reflected her inner turmoil as she found a seat among us. She sank into a plush armchair, clasping her hands together in her lap. Her glance drifted to the crackling fireplace, and she was lost in thought.

Breanna, ever wise, broke the stillness. "Holli, what did your brother say? Is he willing to explain why he wants to sign that contract?"

Holli let out a weary sigh, her fingers tapping a nervous rhythm on her thigh. "Steve," she began, "he's convinced this is our family's way out of economic trouble. You see, he's been struggling for years now. His practice went under, and making ends meet has been a constant battle. He had to take out loans to cover medical bills when his wife fell ill, and those debts have been mounting ever since. His mortgage payments are overdue, and the threat of foreclosure looms over him. It's like he's drowning in financial despair. Steve believes selling the property to Kensington is the only solution, but I'm not sure it's the right way."

"I think we need to approach this strategically," I suggested. "Given Steve's current state of mind and economic pressure, we can't simply ask him not to sign the deal. It's important to acknowledge his concerns and offer an alternative."

Holli said, "We also need to play into his attorney persona. Steve is someone who values evidence, facts, and due process. He might be more inclined to listen if we frame our request in those terms."

Rebeccah's eyes brightened with hope as she grasped the potential of this approach. "So, what are you suggesting?"

Holli outlined the strategy, "We propose that Steve waits to sign the contract until we have all the evidence beyond a reasonable doubt. Kensington is either guilty or not guilty of any despicable intent. This allows us to satisfy his desire for due process while buying us the time to investigate."

Samantha added, "During this time, we continue to dig into Kensington's activities, looking for evidence of their true intentions. We need concrete proof to present to Steve."

Holli's relief was evident. "I'll talk to Steve and present this plan to him. I'll emphasize that it's not about rushing into a decision but about ensuring we make an informed one."

"Let's call it a night," I suggested. "We'll continue our cyber investigation tomorrow and contact Joshua Peele. We need a clearer picture."

Breanna and Holli nodded. Samantha was ready to dive into the virtual realm again. "I'll make sure to sift through every byte of data we have. There might be hidden connections we've missed."

Holli, her eyes heavy with both exhaustion and worry for her family's land, stood up. "I'll go make that call to my brother now. I hope he goes for this idea of waiting until we have all the facts."

Holli left the room to converse with her brother, and Samantha began setting up her digital workspace again. Her fingers traced patterns on her notebook. Breanna looked contemplative.

"Let's reconvene in the morning," I said.

Chapter 5

The morning air at Evergreen Haven Lodge was crisp and refreshing, carrying the earthy scent of pine trees and the distant promise of adventure. As I made my way from my room to the lodge's dining area, the sun had just begun its ascent, casting a warm, golden glow over the rustic interior.

The sight that greeted me was a heartwarming one. My friends, Breanna, Samantha, Holli, and April, were already seated around the large wooden table, their faces illuminated by the soft morning light streaming through the windows. They were engaged in animated conversation, their voices filled with laughter and camaraderie.

With her notebook and pen, Breanna detailed some new insights she had uncovered during her late-night research. At the same time, Samantha, her laptop open and ready, was eager to dive into the digital investigation. Holli discussed her plans to call her brother again for more information about the contract. With his warm smile and easygoing demeanor, Seth was fully integrated into our group, a steadfast presence that had become increasingly familiar.

The smells wafting from the kitchen were equally enticing. The aroma of freshly brewed coffee mingled with the irresistible scent of sizzling bacon and homemade pancakes, courtesy of the lodge's chef. The breakfast promised comfort and sustenance, a perfect start to the day's endeavors.

With a smile on my face and a sense of gratitude in my heart, I approached the table to join my friends. Their laughter subsided as they noticed my arrival, and warm greetings filled the air. As I settled into my chair, I couldn't help but feel a profound sense of purpose among us. We were a diverse group brought together to uncover the mysteries surrounding Kensington Corporation and protect the beauty of Kodiak.

Feeling the weight of our investigation and the complex web of secrets surrounding Kensington Corporation, I decided it was time to change the scenery. We needed to clear our minds and gain a fresh perspective, and what better way to do that than by immersing ourselves in the natural beauty that Evergreen Haven Lodge provided.

I addressed my companions with a newfound sense of purpose, "How about we all hike to clear our minds and get a fresh perspective? The beauty of this place might inspire us and reveal something new."

Excitement filled the room as my suggestion met a unanimous agreement. The prospect of stepping out into the pristine wilderness surrounding the lodge was invigorating, a chance to temporarily set aside our digital investigations and legal analyses.

We quickly made our way to our rooms to change into more suitable attire for the hike. The air filled with anticipation as we exchanged knowing glances, eager to explore the untouched landscape of Kodiak.

We set off on the "Wilderness Explorer Trail," a renowned and picturesque trailhead outside Evergreen Haven Lodge. This trail offered a captivating odyssey through Kodiak's pristine wilderness, granting us a welcome escape from our intense investigations. It was the perfect path for our expedition. April kindly returned to the lodge, leaving us to venture forth.

As we gathered outside, the morning sunlight filtered through the tall trees, casting dappled shadows on the forest floor. The sounds of nature enveloped us – the gentle rustling of leaves, the distant call of birds, and the soothing murmur of a nearby stream.

With each step we took along the forest trail, the air seemed to grow fresher, and the worries that weighed on our minds began dissipating. The beauty of Evergreen Haven Lodge's surroundings was a balm for the soul, a reminder of the preciousness of the wilderness we were determined to protect.

As we ventured deeper into the forest, the path led us to a serene clearing by the lake. The sight took our breath away – the pristine water glistened under the sun's gentle caress, surrounded by a carpet of wildflowers in a riot of colors. It was a moment of pure serenity, a scene that seemed to exist outside of time.

Breanna, her notebook temporarily forgotten, breathed in deeply, her face illuminated by a radiant smile. "This place is incredible," she remarked, her voice filled with wonder.

Holli's gaze on the tranquil lake added, "It's moments like these that remind us why we're fighting so hard to protect it."

Samantha couldn't resist snapping pictures of the breathtaking landscape, capturing the essence of Kodiak's untouched beauty.

As our hike continued, the excitement still pulsed through us, even as we spoke about our ongoing investigation. But then, something caught my eye, causing me to double-take. A building nestled among the trees just off the path, an unexpected sight in the forest's heart. I called the others, and with a shared sense of curiosity, we diverted from the trail and headed toward the mysterious structure, eager to explore the secrets it might hold.

Thanks to the cushioning pine needles beneath our feet, a hush enveloped our footsteps as we approached the enigmatic forest building. The structure bore the marks of time's relentless passage, its weathered facade a testament to its years of solitude in the woods. I watched as Holli reached the door first. With a firm grip on the timeworn handle, she pushed the door open, the hinges protesting with a distinctive creak. A dim, uncertain light emanated from within, and our eyes met in shared emotions of both anticipation and caution.

As we stepped inside, the air was thick with the musty scent of aged wood. The room was a time capsule filled with relics of the past. Dusty bookshelves lined one wall, their contents long untouched. Tattered maps adorned another, hinting at journeys long forgotten. In the center of the room, an ornate desk stood, covered in a layer of dust, its surface adorned with scattered papers.

Breanna couldn't resist the urge to investigate. She carefully picked up one of the papers, her eyes widening as she read them. "This is a ledger," she said, her voice filled with awe. "It dates back decades. It seems to be a record of lodge guests, but there's more here."

Samantha wasted no time. She pulled out her phone and began photographing the ledger, her fingers dancing across the screen. "This is a significant find," she remarked. "It might contain clues about the lodge's history and connection to Kensington."

Still near the door, Holli was captivated by a series of old photographs hanging on the wall. They depicted scenes from the lodge's past, guests engaged in outdoor adventures, and the surrounding pristine wilderness. She pointed to one particular photo. "Look at this," she exclaimed. "It's a group of people, and one of them looks like Joshua Peele."

We gathered around the photograph, studying the faces, and sure enough, there he was, a younger Joshua Peele among a group of individuals. The discovery sent a shiver down our spines, further solidifying the connection between Kensington Corporation and Evergreen Haven Lodge.

Our exploration of the building led us to discover a trove of documents, photographs, and relics from the lodge's past story. Each item we uncovered added a new layer to the intricate puzzle we were determined to solve, immersing us further in the mysteries surrounding Kensington's connection to this place. However, one detail stood out as peculiar amidst the old and forgotten. Among the layers of dirt and dust, I noticed fresh footprints imprinted as if someone had been there not too long ago. The question loomed: who had ventured into this hidden building, and what had drawn them here?

With a sense of purpose and a trove of newfound information, we left the building for now, returning to the hiking trail. The forest seemed different, more alive with the weight of history, as if the trees themselves held past secrets. As we hiked back to Evergreen Haven Lodge, the excitement of our discovery buzzed in the air.

Back at Evergreen Haven Lodge, we gathered around a wooden table in the great room, our faces illuminated by the soft glow of the room's warm lighting. Samantha had meticulously documented the ledger and the photographs from the hidden building, her phone now displaying a digital archive of our findings.

Breanna, still clutching the ledger, began to share her insights. "The ledger is a goldmine of information. It not only lists the lodge's guests but also contains notes about significant events and transactions. There are references to meetings involving prominent figures, including a few that mention Joshua Peele."

Samantha chimed in, her fingers tapping on her phone. "And these photographs, especially the one with Joshua Peele, provide visual evidence of his historical connection to Evergreen Haven Lodge. This strengthens our case that Kensington's interest in the lodge goes way back."

Still reflecting on our discovery in the forest building, Holli added, "It's like we stumbled upon a hidden chapter of Kodiak's history, one concealed deliberately. But why? What does Kensington have to hide?"

I leaned forward, my mind racing with the implications of our findings. "We must dig deeper into these historical records and cross-reference them with Kensington Corporation's activities. There might be a pattern or motive within."

Samantha nodded, her eyes gleaming with determination. "I'll get to work on that right away. With our information, I can search for connections or overlaps between the lodge's history and Kensington's operations."

As Samantha embarked on her digital investigation, we turned our attention to the photographs we had found. Each image told a story, and we began to piece together a timeline of the lodge's past. The faces in the pictures were not just nameless guests; they were individuals who had left their mark on Evergreen Haven Lodge.

Breanna pointed to a photograph of a group gathered around a bonfire. "This one seems significant," she said. "There's a date on the back—1967. That was the same year Kensington Corporation acquired the lodge. And look, Joshua Peele is there again."

Holli leaned closer, studying the people in the photograph. "We need to find out who these other individuals are. They might hold the key to understanding what transpired during that time."

Our discussion was interrupted by the soft chime of Samantha's tablet. She turned it to face us, her eyes wide with astonishment. "You won't believe what I've found," she said.

A document on her tablet screen was seemingly unrelated to Evergreen Haven Lodge or Kensington Corporation. It was an old newspaper article from 1967, the same year of Kensington's lodge acquisition. The headline read, "Kensington Corporation's Controversial Venture: The Kodiak Dam Project."

My heart raced as I read those words. The article detailed how Kensington had faced strong opposition from environmental groups and the local community for its proposed dam project on Kodiak Island. The controversy had overshadowed their acquisition of Evergreen Haven Lodge.

Breanna's eyes widened in realization. "This could be the distraction we've been looking for. While the public focused on the dam project, Kensington might have been up to something else entirely with the lodge."

As we contemplated the implications of this discovery, Samantha continued her explanation. "This article doesn't provide many details about the dam project, but it does mention that Joshua Peele was the lead executive for Kensington at the time. It seems he was at the center of the lodge's acquisition and the dam project."

Holli's voice held a note of urgency. "We need to find out what happened with that dam project and if it's connected to the lodge. It could be the key to understanding Kensington's true intentions."

With newfound determination, we divided our tasks. Samantha would delve deeper into the dam project's history, searching for any connections to Evergreen Haven Lodge. Holli would continue to scrutinize the ledger and the photographs for additional clues. Breanna and I decided to revisit Joyce Williams, hoping she might have information about the dam project.

Hurrying back, a swift hike drove our momentum to put our plans into action. The renewed determination surged through us, stronger than ever. The distractions and misleading trails only fueled our resolve to unveil the truth, driving us forward without hesitation.

We made our way back to Evergreen Haven Lodge and its great room. I saw April enter and sat down at one of the chairs located by the fireplace. Breanna and I looked at each other with a shared sense of purpose. We believe revisiting the Kodiak Historical Society might yield more information about Kensington Corporation's historical ties to Evergreen Haven Lodge.

"Hey, April," I called out, gesturing for her to join us. "Breanna and I are planning to return to the Historical Society to dig deeper into Kensington's history here. Want to come along?"

April hesitated momentarily, her gaze shifting between us and the stack of documents she had been reviewing. Her involvement in our investigation had grown more significant by the day, but her stakes were higher.

"I appreciate the offer," April replied, her voice calm but tinged with uncertainty, "but I think I should continue looking into Kensington's activities from a different angle.

Upon hearing April's decision, I maintained a thoughtful expression, my features revealing a blend of understanding and respect. My eyes conveyed a sense of acknowledgment as I listened to her response. While a touch of disappointment coursed through me, knowing April wouldn't be joining us on this particular leg of the investigation, my demeanor remained supportive. I recognized the significance of April's connection to the situation and trusted her judgment. I knew our friend was making a difficult decision that was best for her.

Emotions ran high as Breanna and I made our way to the Kodiak Historical Society, our footsteps echoing off the familiar wooden floors. The scent of aged paper and the sense of history filled the air, serving as a poignant reminder of the mysteries we were attempting to unravel.

Joyce Williams greeted us with a warm smile as we entered the small but cozy space dedicated to Kodiak's rich history. She was instrumental in yesterday's visit, helping us uncover vital information about Evergreen Haven Lodge's past and its connection to Kensington Corporation. Her presence reassured us as we embarked on this crucial research journey again.

"We're back," Breanna announced with a determined nod, her notebook clutched. "We must dive deeper into the Kensington Dam Project and its historical context."

Joyce's eyes sparkled with curiosity and a genuine eagerness to assist. "I'm always thrilled to help those interested in our town's history. Follow me."

As we followed Joyce to the rows of meticulously organized archives, the atmosphere grew thick with the fragrance of old books and the faint rustling of paper. The soft, golden glow of sunlight streamed through the windows, casting a warm, nostalgic aura over the room.

Joyce stopped before a collection of files and ledgers, her fingers gliding gracefully over the aged pages. "The Kensington Dam Project," she began, her voice holding the weight of historical significance.

"That was a contentious issue in Kodiak's past that left a mark on the community."

Breanna, always the diligent researcher, began to scan the entries in a ledger, reading them aloud for our benefit. "The Kensington Dam Project was proposed in the late 1960s to control water resources in the region. They experienced fierce opposition from environmental activists and residents concerned about the impact on the ecosystem."

Joyce continued, "The opposition to the Kensington Dam Project was a diverse coalition of passionate environmental activists, residents, and nature enthusiasts. They were an eclectic mix of individuals who shared a common concern for the well-being of the local ecosystem. Among them were dedicated environmentalists who had devoted their lives to protecting the natural beauty of Kodiak, passionate residents who cherished their close connection to the land, and avid nature enthusiasts who frequented the area to enjoy its untouched splendor. Their opposition was marked by fierce determination, a shared love for the region's pristine wilderness, and a deep-rooted commitment to preserving it for future generations. One of those opposed was Ethan's grandfather, Jacob."

Joyce nodded, her gaze thoughtful. "Yes, I remember those times. Deep divisions ran through the community. On one side, some saw economic potential in the project, while others feared the irreversible damage it might cause to our pristine wilderness."

Breanna continued to search for relevant information, her expression growing more intense. "There were legal battles, protests, and even a few acts of civil disobedience. It was a tumultuous period for Kodiak."

I added, "We're particularly interested in documents or records that might illuminate Kensington Corporation's role in the project.

We believe there could be a connection to their current activities at Evergreen Haven Lodge."

Joyce's eyes widened with understanding. "Kensington Corporation's involvement in the Kensington Dam Project was controversial. They were one of the primary backers of the project, and their influence extended beyond just financial support."

Breanna and I exchanged knowing glances. This revelation aligned with our suspicions that Kensington had a history of meddling in Kodiak's affairs, especially in projects that impacted the environment and the community.

Joyce shared her insights, her voice tinged with historical reverence. "The dam project eventually fell through due to the overwhelming opposition and legal hurdles. It left a lasting scar on the town, a period of history many would rather forget."

Breanna said, "But it might hold the key to understanding Kensington's motives and connections in the present."

With Joyce's guidance, we continued our research, poring over old newspaper clippings, legal documents, and personal accounts of those tumultuous times. The emotions of the past seemed to come alive in the room as if the walls held the echoes of the community's struggles.

As we wrapped up our research with Joyce's invaluable guidance, Breanna and I expressed our heartfelt gratitude, acknowledging her immense help in unraveling the history of Evergreen Haven Lodge. With gratitude in our voices, we thanked her for the insights she had provided and the doors she had opened for us. We then returned to Evergreen Haven Lodge, the journey filled with discussions about the significance of the uncovered information and our next steps. The weight of the revelations lingered in our words, a blend of excitement and apprehension as we prepared to confront the truth lurking within the lodge's walls.

Upon our return to Evergreen Haven Lodge, we found the atmosphere charged with anticipation. Samantha had been busy during our absence and greeted us with excitement and exhaustion.

"Welcome back, you two," Samantha said, her fingers dancing over her laptop keyboard. "You won't believe what I've uncovered."

The great room, dimly lit and filled with the scent of the forest just beyond its walls, felt like a hub of secrets waiting to unravel. Breanna and I exchanged glances, our curiosity piqued.

"What did you find?" I asked, my voice trembling with a mix of eagerness and apprehension.

Samantha spun her laptop around to reveal documents and digital records. "I managed to dig deeper into Kensington Corporation's history here in Kodiak. It's not just the dam project. They've been involved in various development plans over the years, often met with opposition from the community."

Breanna leaned in, her eyes scanning the screen. "This interference pattern seems consistent with their recent activities at the lodge. It's like they have a playbook for how they operate."

Samantha nodded, her expression determined. "Exactly. But here's something to think about. We feel that Kensington Corp wants to build on the land. I was able to come up with a pretty incriminating document."

My heart skipped a beat as I remembered the red herring we had encountered. "You mean the one that hinted Kensington is involved in a new scheme?"

"I don't think they're involved in a new scheme, but rather a re-cycling scheme," Samantha said thoughtfully. We all looked at Holli's parents' property, right?"

We all nodded our heads in agreement.

Samantha continued, "What did we see there besides trees?"

"A lake," answered Holli.

Samantha continued, "Yes, a lake, and lakes always have a place that feeds into them, right?"

Again, we all nodded in agreement.

"It's like Kensington Dam Project, Part II," Samantha concluded, her words hanging in the air, heavy with implications.

We all felt the gravity of the situation, realizing that our next steps held the potential to unravel a web of mystery that had shrouded our investigation. The room seemed to hum with this understanding, with an unspoken consensus that we couldn't let fear or hesitation guide us. In response to the charged atmosphere, Holli stepped into the action role. Her determination and unwavering spirit were palpable, and she volunteered to initiate the call on speakerphone. This choice allowed us all to participate actively in the dialogue defining our investigative path, come what may.

The decision to talk to Joshua Peele weighed heavily on our minds. The room had a mix of anticipation and anxiety as we recognized the importance of this conversation. With a determined look, Holli volunteered to make the speakerphone call so we could all be part of the conversation.

As Holli dialed Joshua Peele's number, the room fell into a peaceful silence. Each ring of the phone seemed to echo our collective antici-pation. Finally, he answered, his voice crisp and professional.

"Hello, this is Joshua Peele speaking."

Holli cleared her throat before speaking, her voice unwavering. "Mr. Peele, this is Holli Bachman. I wanted to discuss your offer for my family's land."

There was a brief pause on the other end, and we could almost hear the gears turning in Joshua Peele's mind. "Miss Bachman, I'm glad you called. I believe we can come to a mutually beneficial agreement regarding the property."

Holli didn't waste time getting to the significant part. "I'd like to understand your intentions better, Mr. Peele. Why is Kensington Corporation so interested in this land, and why do you want to acquire it?"

Again, there was a calculated pause, and then Joshua Peele responded, his tone measured. "Miss Bachman, the land in question holds strategic value for us. We have plans for its development that align with our corporate objectives. I can assure you that our intentions are entirely above board."

Holli, not one not swayed, pressed on. "But what are those corporate objectives, Mr. Peele? And why the urgency in acquiring the land?"

Joshua Peele hesitated, and we could sense a certain guardedness in his response. "I'm afraid I can't go into the specifics now, Miss Bachman. However, I assure you that Kensington Corporation has a strong track record of responsible development and environmental stewardship."

Holli's expression remained resolute, and she wasn't satisfied with his vague assurances. "Mr. Peele, this land is not just a piece of real estate. It holds sentimental value for my family and deep historical significance for Kodiak. I need more than vague assurances."

Joshua Peele sighed on the other end of the line as if contemplating his following words carefully. "Miss Bachman, I understand your concerns and respect your attachment to the land. I assure you we do not take this matter lightly. However, the details of our development plans are confidential at this stage. What I can propose is a face-to-face meeting where I can share more information under a non-disclosure agreement. It would be an opportunity for you to understand our intentions better."

Holli glanced at us, her face a mixture of determination and caution. She then nodded, accepting Joshua Peele's offer. "Alright, Mr. Peele. I'm willing to meet and discuss this further. But please understand my priority. I won't agree to anything that jeopardizes that."

"Of course, Miss Bachman," Joshua replied. I'll have my assistant contact you to arrange the details of our meeting. I believe this will be a productive step forward."

With the call concluded, we collectively let out a breath we hadn't realized we were holding. It was a small victory in our ongoing investigation, a chance to get closer to the truth behind Kensington Corporation's interest in Evergreen Haven Lodge.

As we delved into our discussion about the upcoming meeting with Joshua Peele, the lodge's front door swung open, and to our surprise, Seth walked in. His unannounced arrival was a rarity. The room briefly fell into a hush, all eyes turning to him.

Seth's face bore a mix of concern and curiosity as he greeted us with a warm smile. His gaze lingered on Samantha for a moment before he addressed the group. "Hey, everyone. I hope I'm not intruding. I noticed you hadn't called today, Samantha, and I wanted to make sure everything's alright."

Samantha's emotions were a whirlwind. Seth's unexpected visit took her aback, her usual confident demeanor momentarily shaken. Her voice, however, remained composed as she replied, "Seth, I appreciate your concern. I'm sorry for not calling. Time escaped me."

Breanna and I exchanged knowing glances. It was evident that there was something more between Samantha and Seth than met the eye. Their connection had been growing, and while Samantha often guarded her emotions, her gratitude for Seth's concern was unmistakable.

Seth, ever wise, nodded in understanding. "No need to apologize, Samantha. I understand how important this is to you. Just remember, I'm here to support you in any way I can."

Samantha smiled, a mixture of relief and appreciation in her eyes. "Thank you, Seth."

With Seth's unexpected arrival, our group dynamics shifted once again. The mysteries surrounding Kensington Corporation and Evergreen Haven Lodge continued to deepen, but now, Samantha had an unwavering pillar of support.

Chapter 6

The sun dipped below the horizon, casting long shadows over the backdrop surrounding Evergreen Haven Lodge. The day's revelations left us with more queries than solutions. The mysteries of Kensington Corporation's historical ties to the lodge deepened with every discovery. The promise of an encounter with Joshua Peele hung in the air, an opportunity to unveil the corporation's true motives.

Breanna and Samantha continued their online searches on their laptops. Holli sat in a plush armchair, her eyes fixed on the crackling flames. Seth, the unexpected visitor turned steadfast supporter, connected our group, a reassuring presence in the face of the unknown.

It began with a faint sound, audible over the rustling of leaves outside—a rhythmic tapping, like a distant drumbeat. We exchanged puzzled glances, wondering about the source of this curious disturbance. It wasn't long before we realized the answer lay just beyond the lodge's windows.

We all moved towards the glass panes. The tapping grew more insistent. Our eyes widened in astonishment as we gazed at a sight that defied explanation. The lodge's exterior bathed in an eerie, otherworldly light, and the woods glowed with an unnatural radiance.

Breanna, her voice tinged with wonder, broke the silence. "What... what is that light?"

Samantha grabbed her camera and began capturing the surreal scene. "I've never seen anything like this. It's like the woodland is lit internally."

An unspoken agreement passed between us—it was time to investigate this occurrence outside. The trees, bathed in a greenish glow, cast elongated shadows that danced like specters in the night. The melody, haunting and beautiful, emanated from the very heart of the backwoods.

We followed the light and sound source, and the woodland opened up to reveal a clearing, much like the one we encountered earlier in the day. The transformation was astonishing. The lake that had once sparkled under the sun's caress was now a radiant pool of luminescence, its waters aglow.

The song grew more spellbinding as we approached the lake's edge. Holli, her eyes wide with wonder, ventured closer, dipping her hand into the glowing water. "This... this is incredible," she whispered.

We neared the origin of the strange incident. A tall, bearded man in his late thirties emerged from the woods. He sported the attire of a ranger, and a warm, inviting grin lit up his face. It was Ethan, and his smile beckoned me nearer.

A sense of relief and excitement replaced their surprise at encountering him. He was the perfect person to explain the unexplained event they were witnessing. Breanna, Samantha, Holli, and I exchanged glances, their expressions a blend of hope and curiosity as he drew near.

Ethan greeted them as if he had been expecting their arrival. "Hello there," he said. "You've stumbled upon one of nature's captivating spectacles."

Samantha, always eager for answers, couldn't contain her curiosity. "What is this? What are we seeing and hearing?"

Ethan's eyes twinkled with appreciation for the natural world as he began to explain. "What you're witnessing is a rare incident—the 'Forest Symphony.' It happens only when certain conditions are in perfect harmony."

Breanna asked, "But what causes it? What's creating this light and music?"

His smile grew as he delved into the explanation. "The light you see is bioluminescent fungi, a species unique to this region. They emit this radiant glow as a form of communication. It's like a silent conversation amid the trees."

Holli inquired, "And the tune?"

Ethan's eyes sparkled as he continued, "The sound is created by a combination of factors—the wind rustling through leaves, the water in the nearby stream, the natural resonance of the trees themselves. It's as if the woods are singing its song."

I felt a profound connection to the moment, "Why is it so rare?"

"The Forest Symphony occurs when the ecosystem is in perfect balance when the woods are undisturbed and thriving. It confirms the health and vitality of this place," he said.

We couldn't help but admire and revere the natural world around them. A profound appreciation for the beauty and harmony of the forest replaced the mystery.

I stood enjoying the spectacle with a newfound sense of wonder. Breanna, Holli, and Samantha accompanied me, the symphony washing over us.

Our worries about Kensington Corporation and the investigations faded into the backdrop. We realized the importance of protecting this natural area for generations to come. Ethan explained the event, rekindling our intense love and respect for the outdoors.

"You're committed to preserving this land," Ethan said, "I can provide you with valuable details about the delicate balance of this ecosystem and the unique species that call it home. With that knowledge, you can defend it."

The event indicated the forest's state, a living embodiment of the ecosystem's delicate balance and enduring beauty. A sense of astonishment rose inside me, urging a profound reverence for this natural wonder. The importance of safeguarding and preserving the intricate harmony of the ecosystem emerged.

I let the others carry on with the probe. I wanted to learn more about the woods and the data to help preserve their ecosystems. Ethan led me through the woods, and we began to talk.

"I had no idea there was so much to learn about this forest," I remarked, my eyes wide with wonder as we walked among the towering trees. "It's like a whole new world."

"It is," Ethan replied, his tone reflecting his enthusiasm for the subject. Every plant and creature plays a vital role in this ecosystem."

My gaze wandered to the majestic trees surrounding us. "And what about trees? They seem so majestic. I am impressed with the roots that come up from the ground. Children could play hide-go-seek and be covered by them."

Ethan nodded in agreement. "They are indeed. They're like the elders of the forest, providing shelter and nutrients for countless other organisms."

"It's amazing how delicate the balance is," I mused, a newfound appreciation for the forest's interconnectedness dawning on me. "One small change could disrupt everything."

"Exactly," Ethan affirmed. "That's why we must understand and protect this ecosystem."

"I found a photo of your grandfather at the Kodiak Historical Society. How was it growing up in Kodiak?" I inquired, a genuine curiosity shining in my eyes.

His voice warmed with emotion as he continued, "My grandfather was the most significant influence on my life. In the late 1960s, he was at the forefront of the committee against a project that would have been damaging to this area. It was called the Dam Project.

Ethan's eyes met mine, and his voice resonated with a profound reverence. "His lessons have stayed with me, Rebeccah, and they're a part of why I'm here today, sharing the beauty of this woodland with you."

We sat amidst the natural beauty of Kodiak's backcountry. His bond to this land, his passion for preserving its pristine state, and the wisdom he'd inherited from his grandfather resonated with me. His dedication to the outdoors and the stories he shared ignited a kindred spirit inside me, deepening my esteem and fostering a growing relationship.

I rejoined Holli, Breanna, and Samantha. They had been engrossed in their work all day. Samantha conducted her digital exploration, cross-referencing the newfound ecological insights with Kensington Corporation's operations. Breanna and Holli, unwavering in their resolve, documented every detail about the forest, constructing a comprehensive case for its preservation.

Their warm greetings brought a grin to my face. It was impossible not to smirk; I spent the day with an intelligent, kind-hearted, handsome man. My grin might have been too broad because of the reception it garnered.

"Share the details," Holli chimed in with a playful tone.

Samantha engaged, and her laughter was evident. "Yes, we're dying. An entire day, you say? What secrets did you uncover out there in the woods?"

Breanna grinned and added, "I'm sure you've gathered a wealth of facts today, both about our puzzling woods and... well, maybe a bit about creatures, too."

I chuckled, acknowledging the jest. "Alright, I walked into that one. In all seriousness, it was a wonderful day spent with a remarkable man."

Holli looked at Samantha, "Did you gather any insights we can share with Seth? Something that could help him convey our concerns to the town leadership?"

Samantha nodded with a hint of excitement in her voice. "I did."

We chatted, and the conversation flowed to our ongoing inquiry. Samantha provided updates on her progress in digging deeper into Kensington Corporation's history and connections in Kodiak. Her tenacity and resourcefulness were evident as she detailed her findings.

Samantha leaned in, excitement and concern in her voice. "Okay, everyone, brace yourselves for what I've uncovered. Kensington Corporation's track record in Kodiak is far from positive. They've faced significant pushback from the local community over multiple development projects. It's a recurring pattern – they prioritize profit over environmental conservation."

As Samantha delved into her findings, a sense of unease settled over our group. We exchanged silent glances, each grappling with the implications of her discoveries.

"I dug up an email from Josh Peele to Kensington's top brass," Samantha continued, her tone grim. "It revealed that Operation Land Grab is back in motion, with two potential sites under consideration. The executives have allocated a hefty budget of 10 million for acquiring both parcels of land. Holli, your family's property is one of them, but the other party's identity remains unknown. I'm still investigating."

"I can't help but wonder who's on the other side of this deal," I mused aloud.

"I might have a lead," Seth interjected, his expression determined. "I'll confirm it and loop you all in."

Holli shook her head in dismay. "This just confirms how underhanded this organization truly is."

Samantha continued, "I have also found Kensington skirted environmental regulations or lobbied for leniency in environmental protections to facilitate their business activities. This means that Kensington has environmental violations that are being investigated."

"That is huge," said Breanna. "That means they are willing to pay violations and proceed with progress. We also did not get too far with the Dam Project. I think we knew more than what the historical society knew."

"I will be meeting with Mr. Peele tomorrow. Rebeccah and I will have preplanned questions so we are not caught off guard. He is a smooth corporate talker, and we must be prepared."

"I'm noticing a recurring theme," I remarked. "It is all about the Dam Project. This is coming to life again, but we do not have enough evidence."

Samantha pondered, "Should we concentrate all our efforts in one direction?"

Her words struck a chord. Kensington employed the red herring tactic before, deceiving the town leaders and the community. Could they be using it again? "I believe we should also explore other leads," I suggested.

We all agreed. It was time to take a break and give our minds some respite from the relentless pursuit of solutions. We agreed to go to dinner for sustenance, enjoy each other's company, and share some lighter moments.

I went to my room and grabbed my keys, and we all got into my car. We entered the cozy restaurant in the heart of Kodiak, and a wave of emotion washed over us. The atmosphere lifted our spirits, and the warm, cozy setting was comforting. Jazz music serenaded us, its melodies soothing our senses and suggesting relaxation. The warm glow of ambient lighting enveloped us, creating an inviting, intimate atmosphere.

The scent of delicious food teased our tastebuds, hanging like a mouthwatering blend of enticing fragrances, each telling a story of Kodiak's culinary heritage. The rich, earthy aroma of baked bread mingled with the savory, sizzling notes of seafood dishes prepared in the kitchen. The sweet sweetness from sourced berries added a delightful layer to the sensory experience.

We found our seats. The restaurant came alive with sounds: the symphony of clinking cutlery, the hum of hushed conversations, and the occasional eruptions of laughter from fellow diners. It was a hub of local culture and storytelling where the soul of Kodiak came alive. We were in the perfect setting for our evening, ready to reflect and strategize.

Samantha managed to secure a corner table with a view of the outside. The evening sun casts a golden hue over the water, adding to the captivating setting. They settled into their seats. We couldn't help but smile, finally allowing themselves to relax. Laughter soon filled the air, echoing off the restaurant's rustic wooden beams. It began with Holli recounting a childhood story, her eyes sparkling with nostalgia. She regaled them with tales of her misadventures with her older brother, painting vivid pictures of their youthful escapades that often involved tree-climbing and secret hideouts.

The evening unfolded. The investigation seemed secondary, traded by the joy and shared stories. There was still room for laughter and joy. Glasses of wine raised in toasts to friendship and the adventures they shared, both past and present. They found solace in each other's company, and when dinner finished, I paid the bill. We returned to Evergreen, and the brisk evening air was invigorating.

We reconvened in the great room, still basking in the warmth of their dinner together. Samantha stumbled upon what appeared to be an incriminating document. It hinted at Kensington Corporation's involvement in a separate, illicit scheme that bore no immediate connection to Evergreen Haven Lodge or Holli's family land.

The document, concealed within a complex web of encrypted files and confidential records, suggested that Kensington might be in an unlawful endeavor involving offshore accounts and money laundering. The implications were staggering, leaving us all in shock. We couldn't help but wonder if this was the true motivation behind Kensington's interest in Kodiak.

Holli's concern-etched expression offered a level-headed perspective: "We can't afford to dismiss this, but we also can't allow it to consume us. Let's hold onto these details as a valuable card and continue gathering evidence about Evergreen Haven Lodge and my family's land. We'll be on the right path if we establish a concrete link between Kensington's fascination with the lodge and this overseas scheme."

Samantha had always been our cyber detective, combing through a labyrinth of encrypted files and confidential records in pursuit of the facts. She made a breakthrough that would change the course of our exploration. She had been tracing the intricate web of financial transactions linked to Kensington Corporation, following the money trail from Kodiak to foreign accounts.

Samantha's dedication was unwavering. She delved deeper and stumbled upon an innocuous document buried inside the company's financial records. At first glance, it appeared to be routine correspondence, but Samantha's trained eye caught a detail that sent shivers down my spine.

"I've come across the name linked to the correspondence, and it's something you all need to hear. Brace yourselves," Samantha began, her voice tinged with hopefulness. "This name is a major player in

Kensington's international dealings and had direct access to the hidden funds – 'April Kensington.'"

Breanna inquired, "Do they have a picture of April Kensington?"

Samantha affirmed, "They sure do, and she looks familiar."

We gathered around Samantha's computer, a sense of tension hanging thick in the air as we waited to see the implications of this discovery. My heart raced as the photo materialized on the screen, revealing the shocking reality. It was April. The woman we had been working with and growing close to during our time in Kodiak. She was the heiress to the Kensington fortune. The facts we uncovered could aid Kensington and undermine our efforts.

The revelation Samantha unearthed was a profound tie between the distant scheme and someone among the Kensington family. Her experience in corporate law wasn't associated with Kensington Corporation; it appeared she had a central role in these clandestine financial dealings.

Breanna was the first to break the silence. "Are we sure about this? It's unbelievable."

Samantha nodded, her voice steady despite the turmoil inside. "The document mentions April Kensington, and the connections are too consistent to be coincidental."

The revelation settled in, and I recalled a crucial detail from our previous exploration in the shed. There had been a small footprint, a clue we had overlooked. It all made sense now—she planted the evidence to mislead us. She had been working behind the scenes to divert our attention and create our diversion.

"I'm overwhelmed by a sense of betrayal," I admitted.

Breanna said, "I can't help but feel taken advantage of and embarrassed that I fell for the deceit."

Holli, her voice steadier now, broke the silence. "April's diversion tactics cannot derail us. She may have set this up, but we've come too far to turn back. Let's follow her plan, focus on the false trail she laid out, and investigate those accounts."

Breanna, her expression resolute, chimed in, "Agreed."

Samantha, still shaken, nodded. "We have to play this carefully. Pretend we follow April's path but dig deeper into those accounts. Is there any relationship to Kensington's engagements here?"

Holli connected the dots. "So this is how they've been operating under the radar. It's a well-crafted strategy, and April was their link to the community."

Breanna added, "We need concrete evidence of their operations here, something we can use to expose them to the town leadership and the public."

Our discussions grew more focused as we brainstormed ways to gather the necessary evidence. We knew that confronting Kensington Corporation required overwhelming proof, something that would withstand any legal challenge they might mount.

With a sly smile, Samantha interjected, "I might have an idea. We could have our smoking gun if we could trace the flow of funds from these international accounts to a local project or initiative. It would show that Kensington's interests go beyond mere investment—they have a hidden agenda in Kodiak."

Samantha would continue to trace the financial connections while Holli and I combed through local records and documents. Both of us were looking for any link between Kensington's accounts and tangible projects in Kodiak. Breanna took on the role of coordinating our efforts, ensuring that every lead was explored and no detail was overlooked.

Breanna's eyes widened as she read the message aloud to us. "It's from Will Douglas. He's a reporter who's been investigating Kensington Corporation for some time. He's heard about our efforts here in Kodiak and wants to meet with me. He's suggesting a collaboration."

"Alright, everyone. Time had passed," Breanna began, her tone focused. I've thoroughly checked Will Douglas, the reporter who contacted me. Here's what I found. Will has a strong track record in investigative journalism. He's received awards for his work, and his dedication to transparency and accountability in reporting is evident. I believe he could be a valuable ally in our efforts to uncover the truth about Kensington Corporation's operations in Kodiak."

Samantha said, "We need to be careful about what data we share. We don't know his agenda or allegiances. Kensington is an entity, and they could have influence even in the media."

Holli nodded in agreement, "We can't afford to make any missteps at this stage. Will could be a valuable ally if he pursues the truth. If he's compromised in any way, it could jeopardize everything we've achieved."

Breanna, her curiosity ignited, contemplated the message. "Will claims substantial evidence regarding Kensington's activities in other regions. He wants to compare notes and see if there are any connections. It could be an opportunity to strengthen our case."

Breanna would meet with Will Douglas with caution and discretion when sharing sensitive facts.

Chapter 7

Breanna prepared herself to depart for home to finalize the wedding arrangements. With her big day fast approaching, the enthusiasm inside the lodge was tangible. She shared her excitement about the upcoming days when she would reunite with the women, a prospect that none of us would miss for the world.

We understood the significance of Breanna's appointment with Will Douglas, a journalist involved in Kensington's inquiry. His interest in collaborating with us was a promising development that held the potential to reveal crucial insights into Kensington's elusive actions. She prepared herself to meet with Will, and we congregated around, offering our support and words of encouragement. We wished her well on this critical endeavor, knowing that the facts he provided might be a significant step forward.

"I'm eager to talk with Will," Breanna stated with determination.

I commented, "I'm keeping my fingers crossed that it's related to those foreign holdings."

Samantha nodded. "If it is, I'll be ready to pave a new breadcrumb trail for us."

She went up to leave for her encounter with Will. We understood we would not spot her until the rehearsal. We all got up and hugged and well wishes goodbye.

When hugging Breanna, Samantha asked, "Can I have a plus one for the wedding?"

"Sure," Breanna agreed. "You can all have a plus one!"

"Oh, the pressure," I said, giggling.

A sense of anticipation filled the room as she walked out the door. Holli and I focused on the upcoming conversation with Joshua Peele, diving deep into our preparations. We collected data, compiled probing questions, and were poised to confront him about Kensington Corporation's intentions in Kodiak.

Holli suggested our first line of inquiry. "Our initial question should revolve around why Kensington Corporation is interested in the surrounding property. It's vital to understand their motivations."

I nodded, adding, "We must press for specifics regarding Kensington's projects or developments planned for Kodiak. Transparency is key."

I noted, "We cannot overlook Kensington's historical ties to Evergreen Haven. The timing of their resurgence raises questions."

The atmosphere inside focused on determination, with Samantha hunched over her laptop, her fingers gliding across the keyboard as she delved into her online research.

"Seth," she began, "there's something I wanted to ask you."

Seth turned his focus from his work to her, his expression attentive and curious. The warmth of the sunlight highlighted the rugged contours of his face.

Samantha continued, "Breanna's wedding is in a couple of days, and I was wondering... would you like to go with me?"

Tension lingered in the air, and the room fell into a hush. Samantha's gaze remained fixed. I could see her heart quickening. Seth's response came after a moment of silent reflection. He paused, locking eyes with Samantha, weighing her words carefully. A genuine smile slowly spread across Seth's face.

"I'd love to," he replied.

Holli, at the wheel, steered with a steady hand, her eyes focused on the road ahead. The cafe's front, nestled among the quaint streets of Kodiak, was charming and inviting. A wooden sign dangled above the entrance, adorned with rustic yet artistic lettering that read "Kodiak's Haven Cafe."

An unexpected sight met us as we reached the front entrance of Kodiak's Haven Cafe. There stood April, wearing a warm smile that radiated friendliness. Her presence caught us off guard, as we hadn't anticipated crossing paths with her at this moment. She greeted us with a demeanor reminiscent of a friendly reunion. "Well, look who's here," she said, casual and amicable. I was just in the neighborhood and thought I'd stop by. How's the probe going, ladies?"

Breanna, always one to keep a level head, responded. "It's progressing. We're following every lead and gathering as many details as possible."

April inquired, "Have you found any significant findings yet? Anything that might provide more information on Kensington Corporation's endeavors?"

Always the vigilant protector of her family's land, Holli chose her words. "We're getting closer. You understand the sensitivity of the situation. We need to be thorough."

Joshua walked inside. He was a man in his early fifties with salt-and-pepper hair that spoke of experience and wisdom. His sharp, gray eyes held a shrewdness that hinted at his corporate background, but a warmth to his smile put us somewhat at ease. He began the conversation with a polite offer, a gesture of hospitality in the cozy restaurant. "Ladies, can I bring you something to eat or drink? It's on me."

We shared glances, appreciating the offer but mindful of the task. Holli, with a polite smile, declined on our behalf. "Thank you, but we're here for details and clarity."

He nodded. "Very well, then. Let's talk business."

Holli began, her voice steady despite the nerves coursing through me, "We've been digging into Kensington's history here in Kodiak, and there are few things that don't quite add up."

Joshua's expression remained impassive, but I detected a flicker of unease as he shifted in his seat. "Go on," he said, his tone guarded.

I jumped in, my voice firm yet measured. "We found records indicating that Kensington has been involved in several development projects in the area, often met with opposition from the local community. Can you shed some light on these projects and Kensington's approach?"

I exchanged a knowing glance with Holli, recognizing Joshua's rehearsed rhetoric for what it was—a carefully crafted deflection designed to distract attention from the real questions at hand. "Kensington Corporation is committed to responsible development that aligns with the needs and values of the communities we serve," he said, his tone practiced. "We strive to maintain open communication and transparency in all our endeavors."

To my surprise, Joshua's composure faltered ever so slightly, a fleeting expression of unease crossing his features before he quickly regained control. "I'm afraid I can't comment on specific land acquisitions," he said, his voice tight with tension. "But I can assure you that Kensington's intentions are always in the community's best interest."

"Are you ready to tell me Kensington's plans for my family's property?" Holli persisted, her tone edged with determination.

He responded promptly, "As I mentioned over the phone, without a signed non-disclosure agreement, I'm unable to disclose any specifics regarding the land's intended use. Do you have any other questions for me?"

Holli sighed in frustration, "I guess not. I'm not signing any NDA."

"Very well, ladies, it's been a pleasure," he remarked before rising from his seat and exiting the cafe.

My frustration was evident in the exasperated huff that escaped my lips. "Holli," I began, "I can't believe how he handled our questions. It's like he's been taking lessons in dodging. He's all confident and talks like a diplomat, but every word felt rehearsed."

Holli's eyes widened. "They were rehearsed."

I shook my head, irritation still coursing through me. "He waxed poetic about Kensington's undying love for the environment and promised they wouldn't harm a single tree. We tried to nail him down on specifics, but he'd nod, acknowledge the question, and then, swoosh, steer the discussion elsewhere."

Holli chuckled. "It was the classic political dance. Never really answered anything."

My voice tinged with exasperation. "The worst part? He repeated the phrases like he thought they'd hypnotize us into submission."

"Right," she said. "He used all this diplomatic language, making it sound like he's addressing our concerns without actually committing to anything concrete."

Leaning closer, my eyes glinting. "We have a master manipulator on our hands."

Holli nodded. "Exactly my thoughts. It's clear we're up against someone experienced, guarding those answers like precious gems,"

Samantha remarked, her tone showing frustration and determination. "I couldn't shake the suspicion that April's presence might have alerted him to our line of questioning."

Frustration simmered beneath the surface, leaving us with little more vague replies. I refused to be disheartened.

I remembered another individual Joshua targeted land—Liz Duncan. Her name was mentioned by Seth in connection with Kensington's relentless real estate acquisitions. I recalled that Kensington Corporation had been pursuing Liz's property near Evergreen Haven Lodge, and her staunch resistance harvested attention from environmental activists and the local community alike.

Beside me, Holli had been observant, her sharp eyes catching something I missed. She leaned in and whispered, "Rebeccah, did you notice that? April wasn't here to speak with Joshua. She was seeing that woman over there!"

I followed Holli's gaze, and it all became clear. With her back to us, April was in an animated discussion with Liz Duncan, who stopped a short distance away. Our fascination deepened. It was a revelation that sparked more questions than answers. Why was April talking with her, and what did they discuss?

We settled into the car, and a heavy silence lingered between us, punctuated only by the soft hum of the engine.

The journey back to Evergreen Haven Lodge was a whirlwind of emotions. Holli's determination radiated from her, evident in the intensity of her grip on the steering wheel. Her dedication to uncovering something that would dissuade her brother from selling their family's land to Kensington Corporation remained unshakable. It wasn't about the lodge; it was a task to maintain her family's heritage and the pristine remote areas of Kodiak.

The car sped along the winding road toward Evergreen Haven Lodge, and my phone suddenly chimed with the familiar tone of an incoming text message. I fumbled to retrieve my phone from my bag, my heart quickening with anticipation. The message was from Breanna, and I sensed a rush of emotions. It was brief and to the point.

"Hey, Rebeccah! I just met with Will. He has some incredible info about Kensington. I talked with Samantha, and she has all the details. I can't wait to share it with you all. See you at the wedding! "

We entered the lodge, and Samantha and Seth were hunched over Samantha's computer, engrossed in their work. It was as if they had entered a realm of intense activity and focus.

Holli initiated the discussion. Holli sat beside Samantha and Seth. "Breanna's interview with Will Douglas is a significant step for us. He's been investigating Kensington Corporation, and his willingness to collaborate with us may provide invaluable insights." She let out a deep sigh.

I commented, looking at Holli, "What's your take on why Will wants to be a part of this?"

Seth shared her thoughts, saying, "Will's reasons might be layered. A deep commitment to justice and environmental causes may motivate him to uncover the truth about Kensington Corporation and its operations."

Samantha continued to type away as she replied, "Will Douglas's willingness to meet with Breanna indicates he recognizes promise in our efforts here in Kodiak, so his involvement is a positive sign."

Samantha also mentioned something intriguing that Will said during his talk with Breanna- GreenIsle Holdings. It was a critical fact he came across. Despite exhaustive efforts, Samantha, Seth, and I couldn't locate anything online. It was as if it had been fabricated, despite its potential to be significant revealing bank records, possible money laundering, and other questionable dealings.

"I'm stumped," Samantha admitted with a frustrated sigh. "We've turned every stone, looked under every rock, and still, there's no trace of GreenIsle Holdings. It's like it never existed."

Holli chimed in, asking the crucial question, "Did Will provide any documentation or leads?"

Samantha looked at each of us, her frustration evident in her expression. She shrugged her shoulders, a gesture of helplessness. "We're at a crossroads here. Do we keep digging for foreign overseas holdings or the knowledge that leads to Kensington buying up property for development? Do you have valuable insights from your meetings with Joshua?"

I sighed, my disappointment clear. "We didn't uncover much. He was quite diplomatic, A notable detail was that Liz Duncan was talking with April, but we're in the dark about what transpired."

It was baffling why Will would provide us with misleading information that brought our probe to a screeching halt. This unexpected twist left us frustrated and perplexed.

Chapter 8

I got out of bed and wandered to the bathroom to prepare myself. I gazed into the mirror. I needed to shower and dress for the drive to Centerville for Breanna's rehearsal and wedding.

My auburn hair fell around my shoulders, styled in a way that came across as chic. A pearl necklace adorned my neck, a family heirloom with sentimental value. It gleamed in the morning light, a connection to the past and a symbol of our commitment.

I couldn't help but feel ready and anticipatory for the day's celebrations. Walking through the hallway, I encountered Holli and Samantha, dressed for the rehearsal. With her laptop in hand, Samantha exuded confidence.

The dining area was in the soft morning light, its panes framing scenic views of Kodiak. Tables were set, with floral arrangements adorning each one. The scent permeated us and was nothing short of irresistible. The tables were decorated with platters of breakfast delights – fluffy pancakes drizzled with maple syrup, scrambled eggs, crispy bacon, and a medley of fresh fruits. The combination of savory and sweet scents mingled in the air, enticing our senses and making our mouths water. Holli, Samantha, and I had gathered around a table, enjoying the delectable spread before us.

Holli initiated the conversation. "It's Breanna's big day, and we should focus on supporting her."

Samantha nodded in agreement, her usual intensity giving way to a softer, more lighthearted demeanor. "Holli's right. Our research has consumed us, and so, but today is a day of celebration. Let's make a pact not to discuss the probe during the ceremony or reception. Breanna deserves our undivided attention and happiness on her day."

I interjected, my voice loaded with conviction. "Agreed. We'll have time to pick up where we left off when we return. Let's be focused on Breanna and support her and Aaron."

After breakfast, we stepped outside, and the brisk morning air greeted us with its refreshing embrace. The sun had risen higher in the sky, shining on its attractive surroundings. Waiting for us by the entrance was Seth

Seth, always the gentleman, greeted us with a smile. He drew close to Samantha, walking alongside her, and with a subtle gesture, opened the car door for her. It might seem like a negligible act, but even such acts can be delightful as they display one's consideration and respect for others.

Holli and I exchanged a knowing glance. With everyone settled into the car, we began our journey to Centerville. The two-hour drive from the mountains of Evergreen Haven Lodge to the sprawling backdrops of cattle country in Centerville was a journey through diverse terrains.

"Let's visit the café! Chelsea is bound to have the juiciest gossip," I suggested with a playful grin.

Samantha remarked, "Maybe the yard gnomes have started a gnome family of their own, and we'll find little gnomes running around, taking over the yards."

Holli's voice conveyed nostalgia as she sighed, "I miss her."

As we drew near to our accommodations in Centerville, the sceneries had transformed once more, with quaint buildings coming into view. The hotel exterior was simple, with wooden accents. A quaint, flower-lined pathway led to the entrance, and hanging lanterns illuminated the path, beaming a gentle, inviting glow.

I asked my companions, "Are we all ready to check in?"

Holli said, "Yes, Let's check-in and freshen up before we head out for lunch."

I suggested, "How about we convene here in 15 minutes?"

Samantha agreed, saying, "Sounds great! Then we can head to the café!"

With a mischievous glint, Seth interjected, "Maybe I'll learn about those legendary gnome-nappers of Centerville!"

Our group entered the café, we realized that Chelsea was nowhere in sight. We spotted the familiar booth where she used to sit during our previous visits. It was a cozy corner spot with a view of the café's entrance. We took seats. A friendly waitress named Chloe walked over to our table. Her eyes lit up with recognition as she looked at each of us.

"You all look familiar. Yes, I remember you. You were here at the town hall meeting," she said. "Haven't seen you since then?"

We nodded in agreement, exchanging pleased glances as Chloe's recognition of us from previous visits warmed our spirits.

"We're friends of Breanna," Holli commented. She's getting married tomorrow, and we're thrilled to be her bridesmaids."

Curious, Chloe inquired, "Oh, I love tuning in to Breanna's morning shows! Who's the lucky groom? Local guy?"

Samantha answered, "Indeed, it's Aaron Roberts, a veterinarian here in town."

Chloe's face brightened, "Dr. Roberts! I took my dog to his clinic. He's such a gentle soul, adores animals."

Wanting to catch up, I remarked, "We used to have some great chats with Chelsea. Is she around today?"

Her expression turned solemn. "I wish I could say she was, but she's not here today. She's been dealing with family matters and had to take some time off. Don't worry, I'm here to take care of you. How can I help you all today?"

A short time later, Chloe came by with our drinks.

I reflected, "Time has flown by. It's hard to believe it's been years since our last visit during the Fredrick incident."

Holli nodded. "Indeed, this place holds so many memories."

I redirected our thoughts, "But today, let's focus on Breanna and Aaron."

Holli lifted her glass of iced tea, proposing a toast, "To love and unity."

We raised our glasses. Chloe returned to our table with a tray of delicious-looking sandwiches and salads.

This moment felt like a much-needed break, a chance to relish the joy of Breanna and Aaron's celebration. We returned to the hotel to retrieve our car, the excitement of witnessing Breanna and Aaron's rehearsal.

We seamlessly integrated with the others involved in the wedding. They introduced us to Aaron's groomsmen. The best man Jared became a focal point of attention. His nerves gripped him as he rehearsed his speech at the reception. Among the other participants, they also met the endearing flower girl, a spirited four-year-old named Remi. Her mother displayed anxiety, hoping Remi would scatter the flower petals without causing a scene.

Holli knelt and complimented Remi, "I like your shoes!"

Remi looked up with a grateful smile, "Thanks, but they make my feet hurt, and I can't run in them."

"I know what you mean," I added. "My shoes can be a pain sometimes. Can you show me how you will drop the flower petals tomorrow?"

Eager to demonstrate, Remi stood up and began to walk slowly, pretending to drop imaginary rose petals along the path. Her enthusiasm to be part of the wedding warmed my heart.

She reached the end of her imaginary petal path, Remi's zeal overcame her, and she sprinted toward the gazebo. Loaded with amusement and slight concern, her mother followed, chasing after her daughter. We exchanged amused glances, trying not to make the mother worry as we set her daughter in motion. Amusement bubbled among us, shared in secret to not upset the running duo.

In contrast, Breanna's nephew, Jeremiah, was the ring bearer. His confident demeanor conveyed that he was in complete control of his important task.

Jeremiah expressed, "This is going to be a breeze."

His mom added, offering some advice, "Just remember, hold the pillow in front of you, not to your side. It's not a football," she chuckled.

Seth winked and quipped, "Well, I love football!"

Jeremiah grinned and replied, "Me too!"

"Oh? I used to play football. I was a wide receiver. How about you?"

Jeremiah's expression dimmed as he replied, "No, not yet. Mom says it's too dangerous for me right now," his voice disappointed.

Seth nodded understandingly, "Someday, though. You'll get your chance, buddy."

Just then, Jeremiah's mom called for him. We walked toward the gazebo. We reached Aaron and Breanna standing at the altar. Samantha greeted them with a smile, "Funny meeting you here!" she exclaimed, winking at Breanna. "Hey Aaron, this is Seth, my plus one."

Aaron extended a welcoming hand to him and offered a handshake. "It's a pleasure to meet you," he said.

Holli took in the breathtaking surroundings. "This place is so beautiful!"

Breanna's gaze fixed on Aaron said, "It's still breathtaking. This is where we had our first date."

Rebeccah nodded, "I remember you saying how dreamlike it was. Who would have known it would be this magical?"

Breanna soon reminded them of their responsibilities. "I think the minister needs us. Let's go meet him."

We followed them, and they looked glowing in their pre-wedding outfits and stood at the front, ready to practice their vows and the ceremony. The floral arch framed them, and their smiles reflected the moment's joy. Feelings ran high as the practice concluded, and they sealed it with a sweet, loving kiss. The group erupted in applause, sharing in the couple's happiness. At that moment, amid the tranquil vineyard setting, Holli, Samantha, and I were moved by the event's significance.

Chapter 9

Ye arrived at the vineyard and parked the car. We spotted small wooden signs with delicate floral arrangements, and elegant calligraphy pointed the way. They led us along a scenic path lined with tall, swaying grasses, guiding visitors toward the heart of the vineyard where the ceremony would take place.

Around us, their footsteps hushed on the well-trodden course. Some carried thoughtful gifts and cards for the bride and groom, while others chatted animatedly, sharing stories and amusement. We rounded a gentle curve in the path, and the full grandeur of the vineyard's beauty unfolded before us. Rows of white chairs are arranged, creating a serene and elegant setting.

Samantha looked at Seth. "I would go and find a great place to sit."

Seth sat in a chair perfectly positioned before Samantha for the ceremony.

I asked a worker, "Excuse me, where is the bride's room?"

She kindly pointed and replied, "It's just through those doors across the way."

"Thank you," Holli expressed.

We followed the directions to a small, intimate room. Our breaths collectively caught as we laid eyes on Breanna, the bride-to-be, standing at the heart of the room. She was a delicate vision in her wedding dress.

"Oh my..." Samantha couldn't help but grin as she beheld her dear friend.

Holli included, "You are an absolute vision. This dress suits you. You look stunning."

"Indeed," I commented, "Aaron is a lucky man."

Her gown, embellished with intricate lace details and a flowing train, was tailor-made for her. Tears welled up in our eyes as heartfelt smiles exchanged glances.

She beamed and responded, "I'm the fortunate one. Aaron is the best! I can't wait to be his wife."

Our discussion with Breanna meandered through laughter, emotional recollections, and reflections on our first meeting.

The room became a flurry of activity as Samantha, Holli, and I assisted with any last-minute preparations. We adjusted her veil, ensured her gown flowed, and ensured every detail was in place for her grand entrance. Our roles were as supportive friends and dedicated attendants, all while sharing in Breanna's excitement.

The moment had arrived for us to process down the aisle before taking our places up front. Remi, magnificent in her outfit, was poised and ready for her crucial task of scattering rose petals. Her basket, decorated with white petals, matched her attire. I gave her a playful wink, and she responded with a heartwarming smile. Jeremiah stood, prepared for his turn to walk down the aisle.

Holli took the lead as the music began to play, signaling the start of the processional. She glided down the aisle with a radiant smile, a captivating elegance and poise. I was next in line, a broad smile gracing my face. It was Jeremiah and Remi's turn, two newfound friends whose company we were delighted to have. Samantha made her entrance and walked down to the front. Breanna, the star of the day, began her journey down the aisle, the embodiment of bridal radiance.

Breanna was a well-known figure in Centerville, anchoring the morning news. She entered, and a collective gasp swept through the crowd. She was stunning. My gaze shifted to Aaron, standing at the altar, and it was unmistakable how he loved her. His eyes welled up with tears, his nervousness betrayed only by his fidgeting hands.

They were at the altar, clasping hands. Throughout the ceremony, their eyes remained locked on each other, unwavering. They proceeded through the vows, the exchange of rings, and a brief message without ever breaking eye contact, a profound witness to the depth of their love for one another.

The moment came, "You may now kiss the bride!" the minister announced. There were cheers and laughter as he kissed her for the first time as husband and wife. The two walked up the aisle, and the event's tone changed from a solemn moment to a celebration. The attendees made their way to the barn reception area. The vineyard's rustic charm enhanced the enchantment of the occasion, with tables enhanced in maroon and white decorations and lots of roses.

Breanna and Aaron curated a menu showcasing the vineyard's culinary expertise. The cuisine struck a harmonious balance between refinement and rustic allure, mirroring the enchanting surroundings.

The evening unfolded, it resonated with joyous chuckles and dancing. Samantha, the Maid of Honor, took the microphone with a bright smile, capturing the attendees' attention.

"I have known Breanna for a long time, and we have shared some hilarious moments, like the infamous Cookie Catastrophe. This one time, we attempted to bake cookies for a school fundraiser. Let's say those cookies resembled hockey pucks more than edible treats," Samantha joked, drawing chuckles from the audience. "There was the Karaoke Conundrum. We thought hitting the local bar for karaoke night would be a brilliant idea. Now, the problem wasn't going to the bar; it was when we decided to showcase our 'singing' talents. I'm telling you, folks, we had all the dogs in town howling that night! Our off-key notes were so sharp that they sounded flat, leaving everyone laughing."

Laughter filled the room as Samantha recounted these humorous anecdotes, but she skillfully transitioned into a more serious tone as she continued her speech.

"Ladies and gentlemen," Samantha began. "I have the incredible privilege of standing here today as Breanna's Maid of Honor. I've had the privilege of witnessing the remarkable woman she is, and I want to share a few words about the qualities that make her so unique.

Tears began to appear in her eyes, and she continued, "Breanna is a force of nature. She's the kind of person who lights up a room with her presence, not just because of her stunning beauty but her incredible warmth and charisma. She has a smile that can brighten even the darkest days and a heart that's as they come."

Samantha moved her hair from her eyes; she stated, "She's a woman of boundless compassion. I've seen her go out of her way to help others, whether a friend in need or a stranger she just met. Breanna's kindness recognizes no bounds, and her capacity for empathy is inspiring. She's not just all sweetness and light—Breanna has a fierce determination that's nothing short of impressive. She sets her mind to something, there's no stopping her. This determination helped her achieve her personal and professional dreams."

I began to have tears well up in my eyes. I looked around, Samantha had everyone in tears.

She shared how Aaron had been the missing piece in Breanna's life, complementing him in every way. Samantha's words were about celebrating a union and acknowledging the profound love that had blossomed between the newlyweds.

Her speech balanced humor, cherished memories, and sentiments. Her words had the visitors alternating between fits of laughter and instances of profound emotion, all while highlighting her immense love for Breanna and Aaron.

"To Aaron and Breanna," Samantha said, concluding her speech. Breanna rose from her seat, approached Samantha, and gave her a warm and appreciative hug.

With this heartfelt moment, it was time for the first dance. Smiles radiated from all corners of the room, but amidst the joy, I experienced a familiar buzz emanating from my purse.

Retrieving my phone, I discovered a message from April stating, "We must meet tonight!" A rush of intrigue and curiosity coursed through me. The timing of this message was unexpected. My interest got the better of me, and I couldn't help but wonder what prompted this urgent request from her.

The music played, and the newlyweds took to the floor for their first dance, surrounded by smiles and applause. I decided to excuse myself from the floor and seek a quieter corner of the venue to have a private discussion without disrupting the ongoing celebration. I retrieved my phone from my purse and responded to April's text message in this secluded spot.

Rebeccah: "I'm at Breanna's wedding right now. What's going on? Is everything okay?"

April: "I'm sorry to interrupt, but this can't wait. There's something important I need to discuss. Can we meet at O'Brien's Cafe around 8 p.m.

Rebeccah: "I am in Centerville, about 2 hours away. Is everything alright? Can we meet tomorrow?"

April: "I can wait until tomorrow, and I'll explain everything when we meet."

Rebeccah: "I'll meet you at 9 AM in the lobby of Evergreen Haven. Take care."

Curious about my impending meeting, my mind buzzed. Despite the festivities, filled with laughter, dancing, and heartfelt moments, my thoughts kept reverting to our conversation. Witnessing Breanna and Aaron's joy was heartwarming.

The night grew late, and it was time for the newlyweds to bid their invitee farewell. Breanna and Aaron thanked everyone for being part of their day and exited through a path of sparklers held by their friends and family. It was a magical send-off.

Holli, Samantha, Seth, and I returned to Evergreen Haven Lodge on Kodiak. We talked about April's message and what it could mean. We decided not to worry about it but wait until we could meet with her. We arrived at the lodge, tired but happy, we bid our goodnights. Samantha offered to walk Seth out to say goodbye. I watched from a distance as they strolled together under the starry sky.

The lodge's facade had soft, warm lights that cast a gentle glow around them. Their conversation was light and easy, punctuated by the occasional laughter. Their connection was growing stronger, and how they looked at each other spoke volumes.

The day's events, from the wedding to April's unexpected message, left me with thoughts and emotions. I settled into my room, I couldn't help but wonder what the next chapter would bring, but it wouldn't be long before I found out.

Chapter 10

We engaged in light-hearted banter and reflective conversation, sharing our impressions of the vineyard, the delectable cuisine at the reception, and the heartfelt moments witnessed between the newlyweds. Beneath the surface, an unspoken tension lingered, hinting at the pressure of what awaited us in our upcoming discussion with April. Just then, Seth entered the room, and Samantha's smile widened, her eyes sparkling with delight at his arrival.

Seth settled into his chair. He extended his hand towards Samantha, their fingers seamlessly entwining. Their closeness became apparent, and I exchanged a subtle glance with Holli.

"I can't help but wonder what she going to tell us," I pondered. "Her text message was urgent."

Holli said, "Perhaps she's ready to come clean about those offshore accounts and the pressure she's been exerting on the locals to sell their property. I can't shake off those intense conversations you and I had with Joshua Peele."

Samantha voiced her concerns, reflecting frustration, "Our investigation hit a dead end. Will Douglas provide us with no leads? I'm hoping we can collect some tips from April."

Seth added, "I'm also curious about Kensington's friendly impact on the local community."

"We need to list all the questions we want to ask her," Samantha commented

"I will write a list of what I want to find out and then pass it along, and all of you can add to the list," I suggested

Holli responded, "Good idea, Rebeccah. We can make sure that we all have input."

Holli opened the email and the words on the screen she couldn't ignore. She said She had to call her brother. The agreement attached to the email had his signature, and it raised countless questions. Why had he signed it? What guided him to this decision? Holli's mind buzzed with worry and a growing concern for her brother's well-being. Holli excused herself to go to the room to call her brother.

A deep sadness washed over me. I realized that Kensington Corporation's expansion plans would soon destroy the untouched beauty of Holli's family property.

April entered the room, the atmosphere shifted, and all eyes turned towards her. She was an elegant figure, commanding attention even before she spoke a word. April's face wore a mask of calm professionalism.

Samantha, Seth, and I greeted her with polite smiles.

"Is Holli around?" she inquired.

"She had to step out for a moment," I responded.

"Well, may we find a different room for some privacy?" April requested.

"Of course, but let me text Holli to inform her," Samantha offered.

"Thank you," she replied. "This matter concerns her as well."

We ventured down the corridor, and Samantha ushered us to an available meeting room. She held the door open, inviting us inside.

A few minutes later, the door to the room swung open, and Holli stepped inside, her face etched with bewilderment. It was clear that something surprising occurred during her conversation with her brother, and the moods playing across her face were impossible to ignore.

We grouped around the table, each taking our seats. She sat down.

"I haven't been candid with you," she began with a hint of regret. "I hid my identity to move around Evergreen Haven and Kodiak without drawing attention. My real name is April Kensington."

"We already figured that out," I replied matter-of-factly. "We pieced it together when you left that misleading clue about the dam project in the shed. It only took us a day to connect the dots."

"I was aware that you found out," she admitted, "but I wasn't planning to reveal myself until a bit later."

Holli said, "We spotted the footprints on the dusty floor. It was a clear sign."

"I realized you were getting closer to uncovering the dam controversy from the 1960s. The company responsible was a subsidiary of Kensington that went rogue and began acquiring properties for development. My grandfather dismantled the company led by Joshua Peele, Sr., but Peele kept the organization intact and renamed it EarthGuard Industries."

April surveyed the room before continuing, "I had to stay here to ensure that Samantha and Holli would uncover the truth about the shell companies. Contrary to the ledger, those shell companies were never part of Kensington Corporation. EarthGuard Industries had intricate connections to them. That's why there were so few precise details found in a ledger. EarthGuard never changed the company name in the ledger.

Their elaborate strategy involved acquiring significant real estate while employing shell companies to obscure the actual buyer's identity from public records. This allowed them to engage in conservation efforts, portray themselves as Kodiak's saviors, and enhance their reputation and influence within the town. It was a ploy to establish themselves as local heroes, masking their ulterior motives behind a facade."

Samantha delved deeper into the matter, her curiosity relentless. "So, EarthGuard manipulated this data to incriminate Kensington and push us into launching an investigation against Kensington to drive our attention away from EarthGuard."

April maintained a resolute gaze when answering, "Exactly! Their scheme aimed to initiate an investigation into Kensington while creating an opportunity for them to secure the land for their development projects."

Turning to April, I questioned, "But how can EarthGuard take the property."

April's voice was steady. "The most straightforward approach is through a Purchase Agreement. They offer the landowner an appealing deal, hoping the owner will accept it. This is what they did with your family's property, Holli."

My concern grew as I considered the situation. "What if they persuade most landowners to sell, but one family refuses?"

April explained in detail, "In such a scenario, they would resort to a Land Swap or Development Agreement. By offering it or a beneficial development deal, they make the involved parties a part of the profits from the development. They may invoke eminent domain. This compels the sale of real estate by the government for the greater good of the community, even if the landowner opposes it. It explains why the dam project resurfaced."

She spoke, and the women listened with astonishment and skepticism, torn between trust and uncertainty.

Holli asked, "What about Joshua Peele and my family's property? What about the deal my brother just signed?"

April said, "Let me look at the contract," she requested. "This isn't a Kensington agreement. EarthGuard has been approaching landowners, using Kensington Corporation's name to persuade people to surrender their rights to EarthGuard. Look here at the contract. The fine print states that Kensington is a subsidiary of EarthGuard, making it an EarthGuard deal. I advise you to contact your brother before the land is gone from your family."

Holli gazed at her in disbelief, her self-doubt growing as a contracts attorney. She felt defeated by the oversight. Sensing her distress, I moved closer and hugged her, assuring her that things would be alright.

"Go call your brother and tell him what's happening," I suggested. Steve will realize it was under pretenses, and he has the ethics to guide you in voiding the agreement."

Holli nodded, "I will, in just a moment," she responded, grateful for her friends' support and reassurance.

"Could you please explain what transpired between you and Liz Duncan and why she looked so frustrated with you?" I asked April.

April's gaze moved around the room as she sought to earn our trust. "I had a conversation with Liz right after she met with Joshua Peele. I intended to persuade her not to sell her property to EarthGuard but to Kensington instead."

Holli, looking puzzled, interjected, "Wait a minute. Didn't you say EarthGuard was attempting to purchase all the land for their developments? Why would Kensington be interested? What's the purpose behind it?"

April maintained eye contact with Holli, "Our goal is to conserve the land. We aim to prevent developments in mountain communities, and the endowment funds established by my great-great-grandfather provide us with the resources to do so. This branch of the company dedicates itself to preserving the environment and preventing real estate development that the communities do not wish to develop. That's why I've spent so much time in Kodiak, to understand the community's desires. Kensington Corporation asked Elena Vega to speak here at Evergreen Haven."

Turning back to April, I asked, "What about Breanna's meeting with Will Douglas?"

She took a deep breath before answering, "Will and I have a friendship. He conducted extensive research on EarthGuard Industries. I asked him to speak with Breanna about GreenIsle Holdings."

Samantha replied, "I've hit a dead end! Despite all my efforts, there's no trace of GreenIsle Holdings on the internet. I tapped into all my contacts, even my most reliable source, and still came up empty-handed."

April fixed her gaze on Samantha, "Perhaps Will forgot to mention that GreenIsle Holdings is not a company; it's a codename for the federal investigation targeting EarthGuard."

Samantha's face lit up with newfound hope, and she grinned, "Well, that changes everything. I can start digging into that right away. This revelation could lead us to the crucial evidence we've been searching for."

She responded with a touch of optimism, "I hope so. I know this is a lot to take in, so I will leave you alone until after lunch."

"This will give me the time I need to re-investigate GreenIsle Holdings and uncover any available details," Samantha declared.

Knowing the truth about April's intentions and acknowledging the situation's complexity relieved the women. They expressed gratitude to April for her courage and commitment to Kodiak. They stood, surrounded her with warm hugs, and thanked her for her honesty.

Holli left the room to call her brother. I quickly texted Breanna on her phone, summarizing the discussion's key points and their revelations about EarthGuard Industries. My message detailed the intricate web of deception they uncovered, including the false contracts and the true nature of GreenIsle Holdings as a code for the federal investigation.

Breanna. She expressed her wish to be there with them and appreciated my updates, her unwavering support, and her willingness to contribute, even from a distance.

Holli took a deep breath. "Steve made the same decision I had. He has chosen not to sell to EarthGuard." The announcement was met with smiles and nods of approval.

Samantha reported to the others, "We've uncovered a treasure trove of information related to GreenIsle Holdings," she began. "Among the discoveries, we found concrete financial records that establish a direct correlation between GreenIsle and EarthGuard. There are emails from EarthGuard linking key executives and exposing the fraudulent schemes to deceive people nationwide. There are legal documents that point the finger at them. We've also come across whistleblower reports and law enforcement statements, all of which tie them to many environmental violations, some of which may be criminal."

April was impressed, her curiosity excited. "I will only mention some emails and public records. Where on earth did you get all this information?"

I couldn't help but smile at Samantha's tenacity and resourceful-ness. I turned to April and shared a light-hearted insight, "Samantha lives by one rule: never ask her where she gets her information."

The room erupted in laughter, breaking the tension hanging in the air. It was a moment of relief, a brief break from their discoveries.

Samantha's voice was urgent as she continued, "This company, EarthGuard, is entrenched in unethical practices. They've strived to hide their ill-gotten gains, stashing their money in numerous places."

We knew they were on the cusp of a significant breakthrough.

I asked about their next step, the room fell silent, and all eyes turned toward April. It was a pivotal moment.

Seth's voice cut through the charged atmosphere with a proposal that caught everyone's attention. He laid out his plan, and the room hung on his every word.

"Should we go to the authorities with this information?" I said to the others.

"Probably," Holli said. "This way, we can set up a trap.

"Maybe," Seth began, his tone contemplative, "we could arrange for Elena Vaga to speak at the square in downtown Kodiak. We could ensure that Joshua Peele would also be there, and then we could expose him and EarthGuard in front of the entire community. With law enforcement on standby, we could have them carry him away. I will go ahead and make the arrangements with the local authorities."

Exposing Peele and EarthGuard in a public setting seemed like a bold and decisive move that could bring their mission to a dramatic climax. They considered the possibilities and the impact, and the room's emotions shifted from anticipation to steely resolve.

"This is an excellent plan, and Seth, thank you for taking the lead and contacting the authorities," I said.

"Let's bring Elena into the event," April suggested.

Holli said, "I can tell Joshua we'll meet at the square with the signed contract. That'll ensure his presence. We already know he is as greedy as they come."

"Then it's settled. Tomorrow at 11:00 AM?" I concluded.

"Perfect," April agreed. "The meeting is set for 11:00 AM."

Holli couldn't help but comment, "We always seem to add a touch of drama to our plans."

A shared chuckle rippled through the group as I added, "Yes, we do."

After a while, Samantha, Holli, and I met in the hotel lobby with its rustic surroundings to sit and debrief on what we just found out from April.

"Wow," I exclaimed, glancing at the women. "That was quite an intense revelation. I had no idea we'd uncover a mystery of this magnitude."

Holli said, "It was a complex web of deception beyond our wildest imagination."

Samantha started to say something but then halted, a rare pause in her flowing conversation. Holli and I exchanged confused looks, concerned by her uncharacteristic hesitation.

Chapter 11

I returned to my room after breakfast. I closed the door behind me and began preparing for the upcoming dramatic finish, and my mind drifted back to the beginning of my mountain vacation. I envisioned this trip as a serene retreat—an opportunity to escape my busy life and find solace in the beauty of Evergreen Haven. My initial expectations were the environment, the peaceful serenity, and the promise of tranquility.

My perspective shifted. I recalled my journey, from uncovering the ledger's mysteries to revealing the truth about GreenIsle Holdings and EarthGuard Industries. It had been a rollercoaster filled with adventure, frustration, and unexpected revelations.

With a final glance in the mirror, I straightened my posture and took a deep breath. I was ready to face the day, to stand alongside my friends, and to ensure the land remained untouched by corporate greed. I stood by the window, my gaze drifting to the majestic mountains.

My heart skipped a beat as a soft, hesitant knock at the door came. I wasn't expecting anyone and the unexpected sound filled me with curiosity and apprehension. I crossed the room with measured steps and opened the door. To my astonishment, it was Breanna. She was the last person I expected to encounter.

"Breanna?" I exclaimed. "What are you doing here? I thought you were on your honeymoon."

Breanna's eyes brimmed as she locked her gaze with mine. "I was, but I couldn't resist," she responded, her voice determined. "With everything unfolding, I couldn't stand on the sidelines and let you three handle this alone. Aaron and I booked a room here for the night. So, where can I find everyone?"

My eyes widened, and a smile tugged at the corners of my lips. "I can't tell you how much it means to have you here with us. We're all in the meeting room. You arrived just in time."

Breanna asked, "Can we pick Aaron up in our room?"

"Sure," I said.

She and I made our way down the quiet hallway of the lodge, our footsteps echoing as we walked side by side. We approached the door. It swung open, revealing Aaron standing ready to join us. Our faces lit up with smiles.

Aaron, Breanna, and I made our way to the meeting room side by side. A hushed silence descended upon the room, and a surprise wave flooded everyone's faces as they spotted the newlyweds together. Eyes widened, and jaws dropped in astonishment.

Samantha, Holli, and Seth couldn't contain their smiles. It was as though a ray of hope had suddenly burst through the tension that had been lingering in the air. The reunion with their presence filled the room with excitement.

We exited the building, went to our respective cars, and drove into town. The town square was a gathering place for diverse individuals, mirroring the community's eclectic nature. Amidst this diverse assembly, I scanned the onlookers for any sign of Joshua Peele. Spotting him didn't take long. It looked like he was enjoying the festivities. A smile was on his face, looking arrogant.

Elena Vega took the stage with a commanding presence, her voice ringing clear throughout the town square as she began to speak. The audience fell silent. She started by painting the area's surroundings, her words carrying a deep reverence for the beauty surrounding them. Her eyes sparkled with passion as she described the towering pine trees, the crystal-clear lakes, and the majestic mountains that graced their home.

Elena's tone was a deep concern as she spoke about the looming threat to this wilderness. She emphasized the speed at which it may be lost to those who witnessed progress in development and profit.

She concluded her passionate speech, and a wave of applause and cheers rippled. She stepped away from the microphone, her eyes still shining, and made her way to the side of the platform.

At that moment, Seth took to the stage and commanded attention. His voice projected over the crowd as he began to speak. Ladies and gentlemen," Seth's voice boomed, "I have the distinct honor of introducing four remarkable individuals who have shown dedication to our beloved community and its beauty. These women have pursued the truth and have been instrumental in our efforts to preserve what makes this place so unique."

The crowd's anticipation grew as Seth continued, his words punctuated by enthusiastic applause. "Please join me in welcoming Rebeccah, Holli, Samantha, and Breanna. They have worked to uncover the forces threatening our area."

"I came to Kodiak to escape city life for a while." I began. "I heard about and saw this beautiful countryside during this trip and fell in love. I listened to Ms. Vega and fell more in love with the area. I have also learned about corporate misuse and how they want to take and develop the land and compete for natural resources that make Kodiak unique."

My eyes swept across the crowd. Seth stood beside Peele, without a doubt. It was a reassuring sight, a living confirmation that our plan was advancing seamlessly. I was relieved and determined, knowing that our presentation was progressing. I did not see local law enforcement, which puzzled me. Was Joshua going to get away with this?

Holli's voice carried passion and frustration as she pressed on, her words brimming with emotion. "There are companies out there, as we speak, eager to purchase every piece of property." Her gaze locked onto Liz Duncan, an intensity in her eyes. "My parents were among those who invested in this land, just like many of you, who held these lands through generations."

Peele appeared rattled, his composure faltering. From my vantage point, I Watched Seth lean in, uttering words to him that seemed to inject a sense of fear into the man.

Samantha pressed on, "For the longest time, we believed that Kensington Corporation was responsible for these actions, and these suspicions date back to the 1960s. This company has been engaging landowners in discussions to purchase their property with a unique condition—the land preserved in its natural state. All of this was happening under the umbrella of Kensington's initiative, 'Nature Guardians.' This initiative got mixed up with another one from EarthGuard called 'Land Grab.'" Samantha shared a quick, knowing glance with April.

Scanning the audience, I witnessed various emotions rippling through the townspeople. Confusion gave way to more intense reactions. Furrowed brows, worried glances, and hushed whispers emerged among the group as they processed the revelation of EarthGuard's true nature. The atmosphere crackled with disbelief and concern, like an electric current coursing through the gathering. One woman's face contorted with shock, fingers gripping her companion's arm. People shifted in their seats, their calm demeanor giving way to restlessness.

His transformation was striking. The man who exuded confidence in the café just days ago now appeared ghostly. His once flushed face paled, sweat forming on his forehead, and his hands trembled.

I continued, resolute, "For decades, the people of Kodiak have been directing their resistance towards the wrong company. EarthGuard, led by Joshua Peele, attempted to smear Kensington Corporation's good name while hiding its dark secret. That secret is their ongoing federal investigation for environmental violations. Concrete financial records, incriminating emails, and courageous whistleblowers within the EarthGuard Industries board room have all provided undeniable evidence of these criminal activities. He was at the heart of it all. We will leave it to the local authorities to determine the final charges."

I witnessed Seth handcuffing him, leaning in to utter something in his ear. My gaze met with Holli's and Breanna's, and they returned my astonished expression while Samantha beamed beside them.

The crowd's emotions were palpable as he was escorted away. Some spectators wore expressions of shock and disbelief, while others displayed a sense of vindication and justice served. A wave of murmurs and hushed conversations rippled through the onlookers as they processed the dramatic turn of events.

"Ladies and gentlemen," April began, her words ringing out, "I understand that many of you may be unsure about what transpired. Allow me to enlighten you on the matter. The mountains, rivers, and lakes will remain as pristine as they were when my great-grandfather acquired Evergreen Haven Lodge many years ago." She paused, letting her words sink in; I am committed to championing an initiative that safeguards our natural treasures for the benefit of present and future generations."

She concluded her speech and a ripple of applause began and spread throughout the crowd.

Holli, Breanna, April, and I walked over to Seth. I found my voice first, my tone echoing with sheer astonishment. "You work in law enforcement?" I exclaimed, my eyes widening in disbelief.

Wearing a somewhat sheepish grin, he nodded in confirmation. "Yeah, I should have mentioned it earlier. I'm a detective with the state police. I know I should have been more transparent. I wanted to keep a low profile and avoid raising suspicion. It was a calculated risk."

I couldn't help but tease him, "Well, you succeeded until now," I asked curiously. What did you say to Peele? He turned white as a ghost.

"I told him he was under arrest and that he should listen to what you all would have to say because it will be the evidence used against him in a court of law." Looking at them, he confirmed, "I told you I would contact law enforcement,"

Everyone let out a laugh.

All eyes turned towards Samantha as we wondered if she knew Seth's true identity. Samantha met our inquisitive gazes with a bemused smile, her calm demeanor unwavering.

Holli couldn't contain her curiosity any longer and asked, "Samantha, did you know about Seth's role in law enforcement?"

Samantha responded, "Yes, I've known from the beginning. I'm sorry I couldn't tell you, but I promised Seth I would keep it confidential. He was the lead investigator for EarthGuard."

Aaron raised his voice and said to the group, "Ladies and gentlemen, what better way to celebrate this victory than with a party back at the lodge!"

His suggestion met a chorus of cheers and applause from our group. The idea of coming together for a celebratory meal resonated with us, as it marked a successful culmination and a chance to relax and unwind after the intense days.

The outdoor BBQ at the Evergreen Lodge painted a scene of pure delight. As the sun descended behind the rugged mountain peaks, its warm, golden glow bathed us all in a soft, enchanting light.

Picnic tables adorned with red and white checkered cloths. Families and friends, young and old, gathered around, creating a vibrant tapestry of humanity. Children chased each other in playful abandon, their giggles and shrieks of delight harmonizing with adults' conversations. Elderly couples sat in comfortable chairs, their faces etched with years of wisdom and experience, sharing stories and laughter.

Overhead, festive string lights dangled like luminous stars, casting a warm, inviting glow that enveloped the entire scene. At the heart of the gathering, a roaring bonfire crackled and danced, its flames leaping toward the night sky—the order of burning wood added to the comforting aroma of the BBQ.

The sizzle of burgers and hotdogs from the grill provided a compelling soundtrack to the evening. The air filled with the mouthwatering scent of grilled meats seasoned and cooked. It mingled with roasted vegetables' sweet and smoky fragrance, creating an irresistible bouquet of flavors. A long table offered baked bread, slabs of creamy butter, and platters piled high with buttery corn on the cob. The culinary delights were complemented by an array of colorful salads, reflecting the season's bounty.

In this vibrant and jubilant scene, I stood with a radiant smile. Holding my glass aloft, I sought the attention of the assembled guests.

"To friendship, love, and Kodiak," I declared, my words carrying over the cheerful dinner. "Here's to many more adventures in the pristine wilderness of Kodiak and the enduring spirit of the community. Cheers!"

Epilogue

A year passed, and the time came for my return to Kodiak. I planned to leave work at lunchtime, and it was a moment I had been anticipating. My desk was organized, and my suitcase stood beside it. Nervousness coursed through my veins as I prepared to bid the office farewell.

The prospect of revisiting Kodiak after a year was thrilling. I couldn't help but wonder how the town might have evolved in my absence. The thought of being with my friends for a mini-reunion made me smile. These get-togethers were rare but cherished moments for all of us.

This gathering held significance as Aaron and Breanna would celebrate their first anniversary with us. Their love was unique and heartwarming, making their anniversary a joyful occasion for everyone. The blend of emotions surrounding this journey reflected the profound connection I shared with the town and its people, a sentiment that has grown stronger over the past year.

The clock struck noon. Janet, the friendly colleague sitting in the cubicle outside my office, leaned. "Rebeccah, have an amazing time in Kodiak! I've seen pictures, and it's breathtaking."

I shut down my computer and stood up from my desk, ready to begin my journey back to Kodiak. The office had a subdued atmosphere, with my colleagues busy at their desks, engrossed in their work. I exchanged polite nods and smiles with a few as I approached the exit. The city was bustling with its usual energy. Yet, amidst the urban chaos, I mentally transitioned to Kodiak's slower, more tranquil-paced life.

The two-hour drive to Kodiak was a scenic odyssey through nature's grandeur. I neared Kodiak, and the town's closeness emerged on the horizon. The distant sight of the town square and the iconic Evergreen Haven Lodge evoked a sense of homecoming. I had a heartwarming view when I arrived at Evergreen Haven Lodge and entered the reception area. My friends Holli, Samantha, Seth, Breanna, and Aaron were there. Joy and relief washed over me. I was the last one to arrive.

Holli couldn't hide her delight. Her eyes lit up, and she broke into a grin. She rushed forward and enveloped me in a warm hug, exclaiming, "Rebeccah, you made it!"

With her usual composed demeanor, Samantha greeted me with a nod and a knowing smile. "We've missed you."

"It's unbelievable that an entire year has passed since our last reunion. How is everyone doing?" I remarked, breaking the nostalgic silence.

Breanna said, "I have been doing great and married life is treating me fantastic."

She was glowing with a smile from ear to ear, and she pulled Aaron closer to her.

"I have been busy with work. It just never stops. I miss us being together," Holli commented.

"Seth and I broke up," Samantha said. Everyone gasped, and then Samantha smiled and said, "Just kidding!" It was about when Seth walked up.

"Lots of things changed, but lots of things stayed the same around here," I said with a hint of nostalgia.

Holli nodded, her expression tinged with reflection. "It's been a year since Kensington decided to throw that Defamation Suit at Earth-Guard," she added, her voice carrying a note of gravity. "They're looking at potential settlement in the millions."

I chimed in, my concern evident. "Not to mention the looming Environmental Violations and those sketchy Land Deals they caught up in."

Aaron raised a valid question. "What about the Tax Evasion charges against Peele? Do you think they'll stick?"

Seth's response was firm, his determination evident. "I hope so. The last thing we need is to catch a glimpse of him back on these streets."

Seth's demeanor took a turn as he pulled the small ring box from his pocket. Inside that box lay a ring, his dreams, hopes, and a future intertwined with Samantha's. He phoned me a couple of weeks ago for advice and was waiting for the perfect opportunity to propose during our reunion in Kodiak.

His gaze returned to Samantha, the love of his life, whose radiant smile and sparkling eyes had always been a source of joy for us all. He determined to make her smile.

The time seemed right. Seth cleared his throat, capturing everyone's attention. The room fell silent as he stepped closer to Samantha, his heart pounding. He knelt on one knee, his trembling voice filled with emotion as he presented the ring box to her. "Samantha, we've shared adventures, faced challenges, and created unforgettable memories. You've brought warmth and purpose into my life, and I can't imagine my future without you. Will you make me the happiest person on earth and marry me?"

Samantha's eyes widened, and she gasped, her hand flying to her mouth in sheer surprise. Tears welled up in her eyes as she realized what was happening. Holli and I exchanged excited glances, gripping each other's arms in anticipation.

Breanna whispered to Holli and I, "Oh, my gosh, it's happening!"

With a voice filled with emotion, Samantha said, "Yes, Seth, a thousand times yes!" She flung her arms around him, pulling him into a tight, passionate embrace. The lobby erupted in cheers and applause as they shared a sweet, unforgettable kiss.

Watching their love story unfold, I whispered, "I knew he was going to propose, but seeing it happen is even more magical."

Holli nodded, tears glistening in my eyes. "They're perfect together, and she deserves all the happiness in the world."

We joined the circle of friends surrounding us, congratulating her and admiring the sparkling ring that now adorned her finger.

Breanna leaned in, whispering to Samantha, "We'll have to plan an amazing celebration for you two."

The day turned into an evening. We sat in the lobby of Evergreen Haven Lodge, reminiscing about our past year's journey. Looking around at my friends, I understood our connection was unbreakable. Kodiak had changed, but it had done so for the better. The town rallied behind environmental protection, and its residents were now more determined than ever to safeguard their surroundings.

Our story came full circle. Glancing out the lodge's windows at the majestic mountains, I realized that our legacy would live on in the heart of Kodiak. We embraced new beginnings, and our collective passion for land conservation would continue to shape the town's future.

With a sense of contentment and hope, we raised our glasses in a silent toast to the adventures that awaited us. We know that together, we may overcome any challenge and protect the natural beauty of Kodiak for generations to come.

Acknowledgements

Creating a book transcends the solitary act of typing on an author's keyboard. It's a collaborative effort involving numerous individuals, each contributing to the tapestry that brings forth the mesmerizing worlds an author unveils. This book stands as a testament to that collective endeavor. Behind its pages lies a dedicated and talented team fervently weaving together a narrative brimming with strength, transformation, and the enduring bonds of friendship. To Tiffany Vega, Sara Davil, and Lia Thomas, your guidance and unwavering support have been instrumental in shaping this story, infusing it with depth and clarity. A heartfelt appreciation extends to my cover artist, Sadia Asif. Your creative vision has given this tale its visual essence, breathing life onto its cover and beyond. Yet, paramount among my acknowledgments is to my beloved family. To my wife, Holli, and daughters, Breanna, Rebeccah, and Samantha—you are the heartbeat of my inspiration. Your unwavering love and encouragement have been the guiding light throughout this journey. I cherish you all deeply.

John Russell

Bonus Material InvestigativeSeries Book 4 Clarkston Secrets

CHAPTER 2

The calm waves caressed the sandy shore, and the salty gust promised new beginnings. Pink and orange sky hues seemed to bless our love. Our ceremony was a beachfront affair in picturesque Sunnyville. Breanna, ever the daring and resourceful soul, had been through her union with Aaron two years ago and took charge of planning the entire beachside ceremony.

The sun descended below the horizon, and it embraced the sandy shore. My eyes gleamed with happiness and enthusiasm, mirroring the love that grew within my heart.

I wore a stunning, flowy bridal gown that flowed with the overdraft. The bodice was embellished with delicate lace, and the skirt cascaded to the ground, enhanced with intricate embroidery. My smile shone with love and happiness. I held a bouquet of wildflowers, and my blonde hair blew in the wind. The gentle colors of the flowers complemented the natural surroundings, adding a hint of whimsy to the elegance of the occasion.

Breanna gasped, "Oh my gosh, Samantha, you look stunning! That gown is perfect for you!"

Rebeccah, the sentimental and poetic soul, smiled and added, "Seth is going to be speechless."

Their words of admiration and love only added to my nervousness. It was heartwarming to know that my friends saw the splendor and significance of the gown. Their compliments made me feel even more confident and glowing on my wedding day. Their company was invaluable, and I realized their genuine joy for Seth and me would make it all the more memorable.

Holli touched my shoulder with her serene and poised demeanor. "Samantha," she said, "we've got everything under control. Why don't you take a few moments for yourself? Breathe and relax. We'll be right outside when you're ready."

Rebeccah stated, "Yes, let this sink in. Your journey has been incredible, and you deserve it."

With a smile, Breanna said, "Take a step back from the whirlwind, and when you're ready, we'll be here to celebrate with you."

I gazed at my reflection in the mirror and marveled at the transformation. The woman who had once been a professional and concealed her identity under layers of classified information was now a glowing bride.

The scent of wildflowers from my bouquet filled the room. I couldn't help but smile. The gust coming through the open window carried the salty smell of the sea. I closed my eyes, letting the breeze play with my hair, and sensed liberation. My heart filled with gratitude as I took a deep breath.

The wedding celebration was about to start. Breanna, Holli, and Rebeccah stood beside me, beaming in their dresses. Each bridesmaid's gown mirrored their style and personality, yet they created a harmonious and beautiful picture when they stood together.

Their encouragement and friendship meant the world to me. Their unwavering help throughout the nuptial planning process had been a lifeline.

9 7 9 8 9 8 9 6 3 3 1 4 2